LUCY DANIELS

Monkeys
— *on the* —
Mountain

Illustrations by Jenny Gregory

Hodder
Children's
Books

a division of Hodder Headline plc

Special thanks to Jenny Oldfield
Thanks also to C. J. Hall, B.Vet. Med., M.R.C.V.S., for reviewing
the veterinary information contained in this book.

Text copyright © 1997 Ben M. Baglio
Created by Ben M. Baglio, London W6 0HE
Illustrations copyright © 1997 Jenny Gregory
Cover art copyright © 1997 Peter Warner

First published in Great Britain in 1997
by Hodder Children's Books

A Catalogue record for this book is available from the British Library

ISBN 0 340 68720 7

Typeset by Avon Dataset Ltd, Bidford-on-Avon, Warks

Printed in England by Clays Ltd, St Ives plc

Hodder Children's Books
a division of Hodder Headline plc
338 Euston Road
London NW1 3BH

MONKEYS ON THE MOUNTAIN

The little monkey sat huddled up against the trunk, his legs hunched up to his chin, shoulders up, head drooping. Though he blinked at them and cowered away, he didn't try to move.

'He must be sick!' Mandy whispered. 'Otherwise he wouldn't let us get so close.'

James stepped out on to a branch to take a good look. 'I can see him shivering. He looks pretty weak. If we try to move him, the other two will think we're hurting him. But if we leave him here, I don't think he'll last long. What are we going to do?'

'We'll have to try and move him,' Mandy decided quickly. She held her breath as James sat astride the branch and reached out to grasp the sick monkey.

Animal Ark series

1 Kittens in the Kitchen
2 Pony in the Porch
3 Puppies in the Pantry
4 Goat in the Garden
5 Hedgehogs in the Hall
6 Badger in the Basement
7 Cub in the Cupboard
8 Piglet in a Playpen
9 Owl in the Office
10 Lamb in the Laundry
11 Bunnies in the Bathroom
12 Donkey on the Doorstep
13 Hamster in a Hamper
14 Goose on the Loose
15 Calf in the Cottage
16 Koalas in a Crisis
17 Wombat in the Wild
18 Roo on the Rock
19 Squirrels in the School
20 Guinea-pig in the Garage
21 Fawn in the Forest
22 Shetland in the Shed
23 Swan in the Swim
24 Lion by the Lake
25 Elephants in the East
26 Monkeys on the Mountain
27 Dog at the Door
28 Foals in the Field
29 Sheep at the Show
30 Racoons on the Roof
31 Dolphin in the Deep
32 Bears in the Barn
33 Otter in the Outhouse
34 Whale in the Waves
35 Hound at the Hospital
36 Rabbits on the Run
Ponies at the Point
Seal on the Shore
Sheepdog in the Snow
Kitten in the Cold
Fox in the Frost
Hamster in the Holly
Animal Ark Favourites

One

'*Joto!*' Thomas Nungwi said, fanning his face with his hand. 'It's hot!'

'Mmm,' Mandy Hope agreed. She was lying flat on her back in a scooped-out wooden sailing boat called a *dhow*. Clear blue waves lapped at the sides of the boat, palm trees grew along the nearby shore. Overhead, the sun dazzled. Animal Ark in Welford, Yorkshire, seemed a million miles away.

'What's for dinner?' Mandy's friend, James Hunter, asked. His eyes were hidden beneath the peak of his baseball cap as he sat on the edge of the boat, his feet trailing in the water.

'Fish.' Thomas shifted the sail and headed for

shore. In the bottom of the boat there were three silver fish which he'd caught. He grinned as the wind filled the sail and sped them along. 'Of course!'

Mandy knew that Thomas would not only catch their lunch, but cook it himself. Though he was only fourteen, he had a job as a cook for groups of tourists who went on safari across the scorched grasslands of the East African mainland.

Now though, he was at home with his family on the tiny island of Kima Punju. He'd invited the Hopes and James to join him for a week of sun, sand and lazing about in boats, and they were nearing the end of their first day there.

Mandy squinted at him out of the corner of her eye. 'Don't you ever get tired?' He was on the go from morning till night, always working, always smiling.

'Sometimes. Then I sleep,' he grinned. Suddenly he turned away and listened. He slackened the sail. 'Look!'

She sat up lazily and gazed out to sea. 'What?' The endless sparkling waves danced and shimmered.

James ducked under the flapping sail as the

boat slowed and drifted. 'What are we looking at?'

'Over there!' Thomas pointed. 'Did you see?'

'No.' Puzzled, they shook their heads. The boat bobbed and dipped.

'Yes, there!' Swiftly he changed tack and headed back the way they'd come. 'Keep a look out,' he told them. 'Here come some old friends of mine!'

By now Mandy was kneeling in the shallow boat, gripping the side and keeping her eyes peeled. Even Thomas sounded excited, and he was used to elephants and lions, rhinos and giraffes. This must be something really special. 'What are we looking for?'

Before he could answer, the sparkling waves parted in three, four . . . five different places. Shiny grey shapes leaped into the air, curved and dived.

'Dolphins!' James cried.

They disappeared in a splash of white foam.

'Come back!' Mandy breathed. She hung over the edge, peering into the blue depths. She saw shadows dart below the boat, weaving to and fro.

'Wait,' Thomas told them.

Soon another dolphin broke the surface. He

swam cautiously towards them, his beak-like nose thrusting through the swirling water, his small eyes peering up at them.

Mandy held her breath. She could hear him clicking and creaking, like a duck quacking quietly to himself. 'Hello!' She reached out her hand and let her fingertips trail in the water.

He swam to within three or four metres, tipping back his sleek grey head and opening his mouth in what looked like a wide, toothy grin.

'Isn't he brilliant!' James leaned so far out of the boat that it tipped and rocked.

Thomas steadied it. 'Listen, he's talking to us!'

The dolphin swam even closer. In the background, others leaped clear of the water in playful arcs.

'What does he want?' Mandy could almost touch him. She could see the blowhole on top of his head, the rows of tiny, sharp teeth.

Thomas pointed at the fish on the bottom of the boat. 'Maybe he can smell them.'

'Can I give him one?'

He shrugged, nodded and smiled.

So she took a fish and held it out over the water. Their dolphin swam up to her, bold as anything. He reached up and nipped the fish from her hand. Then he turned and dived out of sight.

'Look what you've gone and done!' James got to his feet, laughing.

Suddenly the whole school of dolphins was circling their boat, clicking and creaking noisily. They splashed with their broad tails, poked their pointed noses up at Mandy, circling eagerly.

She glanced at Thomas, who nodded again. This time she took the two fish and stood up, trying to keep her balance as the boat rocked in the waves made by the dolphins. She held out one fish at arm's length. *Whoosh*! A second dolphin was lucky. He jumped, snatched the fish and plunged out of sight. Then the last fish went the same way. Mandy held it out, a dolphin leaped and took it neatly from her, disappearing with his surprise catch.

'*Who-oa*!' Mandy tottered and flailed her arms. The boat dipped suddenly. '*Oo-oops!*' She overbalanced and tipped over the side as James lunged and tried to grab her. Too late. She toppled and fell into the cool green water.

Down she went, in amongst the dolphins. They came and peered at this strange land creature, twisting this way and that. Surrounded

by bubbles, gasping for breath, Mandy kicked her legs and swam to the surface.

Thomas and James were waiting, arms outstretched. She grabbed hold and felt herself heaved back on board.

'That was fabulous!' she gasped. Water streamed off her into the bottom of the boat. She pushed her blonde hair back from her face and drew a deep breath. 'I was actually swimming with dolphins!'

James wrinkled his nose and tutted.

'Ready to go?' Thomas asked. He tightened the sail and steered the boat to face the shore.

Reluctantly, Mandy nodded. The dolphins had got their fish and made off with them. Now there was no sign of fin or tail or wonderful arching backs as they leaped and played. She sat, still tingling with excitement, watching the white sands and palm trees draw nearer. James had gone quiet, she realised.

'It was OK. I'm a good swimmer, you know.' She wanted to remind him that she hadn't been in any danger when she fell in.

'It's not that.' He screwed up his nose again and twisted his cap so that the peak shaded his neck.

'What then?'

He stared ruefully at the empty floor of the boat. 'That was our dinner!' he said.

' . . . Then we saw them!' James had raced ahead from the harbour up to Thomas's house in the narrow winding street that led to the market-place in the main town of Kima Punju. Mandy joined him as he poured out the story of the dolphins to Mr and Mrs Hope. 'Thomas saw them first and steered us back to take a look. They jumped right out of the water. Some of them must have been about three metres long!'

'Any babies?' Mandy's mum put her book

down and smiled up at them. She and Mandy's dad were taking it easy on the flat roof of the house, sitting in the shade of a palm leaf canopy. She wore her long auburn hair tied back under a broad-brimmed straw hat, and kept the fierce sun off her skin with a white cotton shirt and trousers.

'No, I didn't notice any.' James had quickly got over losing his dinner. His freckled, tanned face was lit up with excitement. 'They were talking!' he cried. 'Making this sort of creaking noise. They're really clever, aren't they?'

'And kind.' Mrs Hope knew a lot about dolphins. She, like Mandy's dad, was a vet, and had studied these fascinating mammals at college. 'If one gets injured, the others will push their heads under his flippers and raise him to the surface so he can breathe.'

'I swam with them,' Mandy told them. From the cool roof-top she had a good view of the small harbour and the sea. 'Not on purpose. It was an accident.'

Adam Hope grinned as she explained. 'Trust you, Mandy. Any excuse to make friends!'

'They'll sometimes come when you whistle,' Emily Hope said. 'Try it. I expect you'll be going out in the boat to see them again?'

Mandy nodded eagerly. 'Thomas says his dad needs the *dhow* to go fishing early each morning. But he says we can look for dolphins again whenever his dad doesn't want the boat. Isn't that great?'

As soon as they'd arrived at the house, Thomas had gone off into the kitchen and left them to come upstairs without him. It was an old house built of stone that was painted sparkling white. The roof was flat, and there was no glass in the windows, only wooden shutters to close at night. The door, like all those in Kima Punju town, was made of heavy, carved wood, studded and bolted with polished brass.

'Don't pester, will you?' Mandy's dad knew her passion for animals. 'Mr Nungwi's a busy man, remember.'

She grinned and promised. 'Don't worry, Dad, I'm going to be just like you while we're on this island.'

'Meaning what?' He looked suspiciously from under his own cap.

'Meaning that I plan to be laid back. I'm not going to dash around doing things. I'm just going to sunbathe and do nothing!' She pictured herself on the white sands, swimming lazily in the deep blue sea.

'Really?' Her dad narrowed his eyes. 'You're not going to chase around studying the local wildlife and rescuing things?'

Mandy was used to being teased. 'Not unless you count rescuing that giant spider from your shower this morning,' she said matter-of-factly.

'What giant spider?' He sat up straight.

'The one that crawled on to your bed and under your mosquito net after I saved it from drowning.' She flung herself on to a chair by the table and took off her hat. If there was one creature on this planet that her dad didn't like, it was spiders, she knew. 'This big!' She made a circle with both her hands. 'With long, hairy legs!'

A look of horror crept over his face. '*How* big?'

'This big.' She made an even larger circle. Then the laughter bubbled up and gurgled out. Soon she was giggling and tickling his neck. 'It'll creep out tonight when you're asleep and crawl all over you!'

Then Thomas and his father, Soud, came up with bowls of rice, vegetables and salad. They spread the table with an orange cloth and laid out smaller bowls, pots of lemon-grass tea, dishes of pineapple, banana and papaya.

'Eat!' Soud said. 'Please, make yourselves at home. *Karibu*! You are most welcome to Kima Punju. Eat as much as you can!'

After dinner, when Thomas's mother and two sisters had cleared the table, Soud Nungwi came to sit with his guests.

Mandy remembered her promise not to pester Mr Nungwi about the *dhow*, though she longed for another trip to see the dolphins. Instead, she took herself off to a corner of the roof terrace and gazed out over the harbour, only half listening to the talk between the adults.

The narrow street below was almost empty, except for a boy cycling by, and an old man sitting on a step beside a wide, carved door. The sun was low in the sky, shining red-gold over the sea.

Looking at Thomas's father, Mandy could see where the boy got his tall, thin figure and ready smile. Soud Nungwi was deep in conversation with her mum and dad, explaining how the islanders earned their living through fishing and spices.

'Spices?' Emily Hope picked up on this.

Mandy turned away and leaned her elbows

on the low wall. Could she spot dolphins from here, she wondered? The sea danced and glittered to the far horizon. No; she realised they wouldn't swim into the enclosed harbour, and beyond that it was too far to see dolphins with their shiny, slithery bodies and tiny eyes. Dolphins with their smiley faces and little squeaks and grunts. She dreamed on.

'Nutmeg, cloves . . . many, many spices. And the farmers here grow beans and cassava. We have lemon trees and lime trees, even iodine trees with gum which we use for medicine.' Mr Nungwi took his time to explain how the villagers cut into the bark and collected the droplets of gum.

James sidled up to Mandy. 'No lions on Kima,' he said quietly. 'And no elephants, either.' Like Mandy, he'd loved the magic of safari on the wide open African plains. 'It's nowhere near as exciting, is it?'

'Different,' she admitted. 'I think they do have leopards somewhere on the island.' There was a forest region in the centre, where there were no roads or villages. Though the island only measured ten kilometres across, it was long and narrow, with plenty of hilly wilderness for a leopard to stalk and catch its prey.

For a while they stopped talking and watched the sun grow fiery red as it sank into the sea. Mr Nungwi explained more about the island; how the spices were sent abroad, how traders from the Arab world had always come to Kima Punju.

'And what does the name mean?' Adam Hope asked. 'Is it Swahili?'

'Yes. *Kima Punju* means Poison Monkey,' Soud told them with a laugh. 'Poison Monkey, after the famous creatures of the Mtondoo Forest. That's the forest by the mountain.'

'Tell us more,' Emily Hope said, as the shadows lengthened across the roof-top.

'The Poison Monkey lives nowhere else in the world; only on this island. Cut off from the mainland for many thousands of years, he feeds on mangrove leaves and eucalyptus and mahogany. He's our special monkey.'

Mandy and James pricked up their ears. This was more interesting than beans and spices.

'But why "Poison"?' Mrs Hope asked.

Soud Nungwi laughed again. 'It's an old story. The local people believe that witch doctors used to take poison from the stomachs of these poor creatures and use it to cast their evil spells.'

'Yuck!' Mandy's lip curled as she drifted over to join the conversation.

Soud held up his hands. 'Don't worry, this doesn't happen any more. But the story lives on. Still, the people think the monkeys bring bad luck. Like I said, it's an old belief, but legends are slow to die. And our island is named after the monkey, so it's hard to forget.'

'And they live on Mtondoo Mountain?' Mandy's eyes glistened as darkness fell. Once the sun had fallen below the horizon, dusk became night almost at once. She gazed across the flat roofs of the town towards the east, at the cone-shaped mountain that rose in the centre of the island.

'Yes. The name means "Mahogany". Mahogany Mountain, the home of the red monkeys.' Mr Nungwi stood and clasped his hands in front of him. His face was cloaked in shadow, only his eyes gleamed white as he took his leave. 'According to the old story, where the Poison Monkey feeds, the trees and crops will die, the cattle will starve and the dogs will lose their fur.'

'Oh!' This time, Mandy's shiver was genuine.

'Don't worry.' Mr Nungwi smiled kindly. 'It's only a story. Really, the monkey is quite harmless.'

Mandy drew her gaze from the mountain to

the group on the roof-top. She looked from one to another. 'It's not *that* I'm worried about; it's the poor monkey. Who could possibly believe that a little monkey could ruin crops and starve cattle?'

Her mum put an arm around her shoulder and drew her downstairs, where the lamps were lit and the shutters closed.

'That's my girl!' Adam Hope smiled. 'Worrying about the underdog, as usual.' He followed them down, telling Soud Nungwi all about Mandy's love of animals. 'You should see her bedroom walls at home; every square centimetre is covered with pictures of dogs, cats, ponies, hedgehogs, piglets . . .'

'These Poison Monkeys,' Mandy said to James, just before they went to their rooms to sleep. 'I wonder what they look like. Do you think we'd be able to go and see?'

'What happened to the sunbathing and lazing about?'

She jabbed him with her elbow. 'I'm serious, James!'

'Ouch!' His eyes twinkled behind his glasses. 'I know you are. But think about it; there are no roads up Mtondoo Mountain.'

'So?' She tilted her head to one side and lowered her voice to a whisper. The lamp on the wall flickered and cast a golden glow. 'When did *that* ever stop us? Oh, James, I'd love to see these little monkeys. Let's ask Mum and Dad first thing tomorrow!'

Two

'*Pole, pole* . . . Slowly, slowly!' Soud Nungwi stood at the harbourside, watching Mandy, James and Thomas climb into a battered Land-rover. He'd been up before dawn, sailed out in his *dhow* and had already landed his morning catch. Now he was helping them to fulfil Mandy's dream. 'The monkeys will still be in the forest when you arrive. They've been there for ten thousand years!'

Emily Hope stood beside him. 'Mandy doesn't know the meaning of the word "slowly"; not when there are animals involved!'

Mandy took no notice. She was all fingers and thumbs as she pulled at the strap fastening on the front of her rucksack to pull out a map of the island. Inside the Land-rover it was hot and dusty. The owner had lifted the bonnet to do last-minute repairs to the engine. Soon they would be on their way.

James had been the tactful one. He'd brought up the subject of the monkeys at breakfast time, as Mandy's dad chewed his way through a pile of savoury doughnuts. She'd kept her mouth closed and her fingers tightly crossed.

'Erm, Mr Hope, we were wondering . . . that is, Mandy and I were talking about it last night, and we – er – thought it would be good if . . .'

'Come on, James, spit it out.' Mr Hope had shot him an eagle-eyed look. 'Do I feel a request coming on?'

'If you don't mind, we'd like to try and find the Poison Monkeys!' He'd come out with it, crimson with embarrassment. 'Please!' he'd remembered to add.

'What about the do-nothing-laze-on-the-beach plan?' Mr Hope had winked at Mandy's mum.

'What about the dolphins?' Mrs Hope had asked.

'We could see them tomorrow,' James had explained. 'Honest, Mrs Hope, these monkeys are so rare we'd never get another chance to see them, would we?'

'It's not that simple.' She'd been sympathetic but doubtful. 'How would you get to the mountain? Who would show you the way?'

'I bet Thomas would.' Mandy had shot in with her suggestion. Thomas was clearing the table just at that moment. 'Couldn't you show us the way to the mountain?' she'd asked.

'What about your mother, Thomas? Won't she need you here today?' Mrs Hope hadn't wanted to be a nuisance.

'And anyway, you still haven't said how you'd get there, Mandy. There are no buses, no taxis, not even any proper roads!' Adam Hope had also tried to put them off.

'Wait, please.' Thomas had gone off to talk to his mother. His mother had talked to his aunt. His aunt had talked to her father-in-law, who knew a man with a Land-rover. The man would lend them the Land-rover for the day if they brought back a basket of lemons from his brother's farm. By nine o'clock, they were down at the harbour waiting for the transport to show up.

'But who'll drive?' Adam Hope had objected as the plan developed. He was wearing his cap back-to-front, a T-shirt and turquoise shorts, ready for the beach, with a towel rolled under his arm.

'I will.' Mandy's mum had volunteered without a moment's hesitation. 'Honestly, Adam, you go and enjoy yourself. I don't mind a bit.'

'Sure?' Mandy had wanted to fling her arms around her lovely mother. 'You're sure you don't want to stay here?'

'And miss the sight of the Kima Punju monkeys? James is right: when would we get another chance?'

So here they were, by the harbour, amidst a busy, colourful crowd of men unloading fish and women in bright red, purple and green robes balancing baskets on their heads and setting off for market.

'It's hot!' Mandy fanned herself with the map as the Nungwis' friend closed the bonnet. He explained the car's peculiar habits to her mum, before she too climbed in.

'He says the left indicator doesn't work and the engine sometimes overheats. Otherwise, it's perfect!' She got in and creaked the door shut.

'It's a bit old, isn't it?' James looked round at the ripped seats and dust-coated dashboard.

In the front passenger seat, Thomas shrugged and grinned. 'Hold tight,' he warned.

Mrs Hope reversed the Land-rover along the harbour, watched by a curious crowd of fishermen. She turned in a tight corner and headed for the road. The car chugged and coughed. As its old suspension rattled over a bump, Mandy and James shot out of their seats.

'Ouch!' Mandy hit her head on the roof, then jolted back on to the hard seat.

A cloud of dust rose from the road. 'See!' Thomas had a firm hold of the door handle. 'You have to hold tight!'

They swayed out into a slow procession of battered lorries and ancient cars, between the women carrying the huge baskets, and children on their way to school. A skinny dog nipped out into the traffic from a dark alleyway, right in their path. Mandy's mum slammed on the brakes.

This time James and Mandy shot forward off their seats.

'Ouch!' Mandy rubbed her forehead. 'Oh well, at least the brakes work!' She was determined to look on the bright side.

Today was an adventure. As they chugged and crept through the one street out of town, she stared out of the window at Mtondoo Mountain, still hazy in the distance. 'How long will it take to get there?'

'About an hour. It depends on the road,' her mum answered.

Soon they were clear of the white houses and narrow alleys, trundling along beneath an avenue of tall coconut palms. Then, after another few hundred metres, the pitted tarmac surface gave way to a rutted dust track.

'What road?' Thomas laughed. 'On Kima Punju there are no motorways like you have in England!'

He was right. On the back seat, Mandy bounced and bumped. A boy on a bicycle passed them with ease.

'Make that two hours,' Mrs Hope said, wrestling with the steering wheel.

'It'll be worth it,' James promised. He too stared out at the green, pyramid-shaped mountain. 'Just think; monkeys swinging through the mahogany trees, eating bananas, little ones clinging to the grown-ups. It'll be great!'

'It *would* have been great . . .' Mandy said dejectedly, an hour later. They sat by the side of the dusty track, still three whole kilometres from where the trees took over from the fields of cassava and beans. By now, Mtondoo Mountain towered over them, but the Land-rover had let them down. Its engine hissed and steamed, as it stood with its bonnet up. ' . . . if we could have made it all the way there!'

'*Pole, pole*!' Thomas said. 'Slowly, slowly. The engine will cool, then we can carry on.'

Emily Hope wiped her oily hands on an old towel, then flopped down in the shade of a nutmeg tree. 'Thomas is right. We just have to be patient.'

But this was easier said than done in the late morning heat. Mandy fanned herself with the grubby map and gazed miserably at the broken-down car. 'So near, yet so far,' she sighed.

'Nearer than you think,' James whispered. He nudged her gently and pointed to a branch above Mrs Hope's head.

'What? Where?' Mandy expected to see a bird or a lizard basking in the sun. She squinted at the tree.

Then she saw a dark face with quick brown eyes and a fringe of white fur. She saw small black hands clutching a bunch of leaves. She saw a long tail and round pink ears. The monkey caught her staring at him and scampered out of sight.

'*Kima*! *Kima Punju*!' Thomas got slowly to his feet. 'All around, look!'

The leaves of a nearby lemon tree shook as another monkey crept into view. He came along a branch on all fours, whisking his long tail. In the sunlight his back was bright red. There was a black stripe across his shoulder, and once more a crown of white hair.

Mandy had time for only a quick look before she heard a rustling in the grass beside her and saw a third inquisitive face peering out at her. 'Oh!' she murmured as the monkey skipped out on to the track, resting one long arm on the dirt road. There, clinging to her underside, was a small baby monkey, who poked his little black face at them and chattered in a tiny voice.

Then there were too many to count; perhaps twelve or more, scrambling down tree trunks or peeping out of the dry grass. Flashes of red, brown and black, long tails waving, little polished nails on perfectly formed hands, and that shock of white hair around the face. They scampered into the open, climbed on to the roof of the hissing Land-rover and peered down at the four humans.

'Quick, have we got anything for them to eat?' Mandy delved into her rucksack for a banana. The mother monkey had stayed close by, head to one side, as if waiting for a treat.

Mandy pulled out the fruit and quickly began to peel it. But Thomas stepped in front of her.

'No, you shouldn't feed the monkeys,' he protested. 'Their stomachs can't digest ripe fruit. It makes them sick. Anyway, it's best not to go too near.' He shrugged and stepped back, showing he was sorry to spoil it for her.

Mandy felt herself blush. In her excitement she'd been too eager to make friends. After all, these were rare wild animals. They had to be treated with respect.

'And these are the famous Poison Monkeys?' Emily Hope had stayed crouching at the road-side. She didn't move as the monkeys jumped from branch to branch above her head. 'They don't look very spooky to me!'

Mandy remembered Mr Nungwi's story about witch doctors and spells. 'No, they're lovely! They wouldn't harm a fly!' The adult monkeys seemed to be just over a metre long from their heads to the end of their long, thin tails. They were delicate, pretty things, with pink-spectacle markings across their nose and eyes. 'They look like little old ladies!'

'If one looks straight at you, look away,' Thomas warned. He seemed edgy that the monkeys were coming too close.

'Why's that?' James asked.

'If you look into their eyes you'll scare them.'

'What are they doing down here by the road? Shouldn't they be up on the mountain?'

'They come down for food and water. In the evening they go back to the hills.' Thomas walked a little way down the road. 'Here comes a car,' he warned, just in time, as an engine roared and another Land-rover rocked and lurched along the track.

'Why doesn't he slow down?' Mandy cried. She stepped to one side and caught a glimpse of a middle-aged driver with a cigarette hanging from his mouth, and a woman passenger sitting beside him. The woman had pointed her camera towards the monkeys and was clicking away before the cloud of dust churned up by their Land-rover's wheels rose and hid everything from view. 'He'll run them over if he's not careful!'

The poor monkeys seemed not to know what to do. They huddled by the road or froze half-way up a tree trunk. There was a shrill '*yow-yow*!' from one of the males in the group. Mandy, James and Emily Hope waited for the dust to settle.

'Idiot!' Mrs Hope muttered, shielding her eyes. 'He hasn't got the sense he was born with!'

'You can say that again.' James was the first to see that it was even worse than they'd thought.

For a dreadful second, Mandy was convinced that the Land-rover had hit one of the monkeys. She felt her stomach wrench and churn. Then she saw what he meant. A thin wisp of smoke curled from the dry grass not far from where they stood. 'Can you believe it? That man just threw his cigarette out of the window!' she gasped.

Quickly the grass crackled and caught light. In the confusion of engine roar, dust and smoke, the monkeys ran here and there, calling out in their chattering voices, giving high, warning calls.

'We'd better move quickly!' Mrs Hope called Mandy to the car with her. 'Here, chuck this on the fire!'

Mandy raced after her and took a plastic can of water from her.

'James, use this to douse the flames after Mandy's poured water over them!' She handed him a heavy canvas sheet.

Within half a minute, they'd raced back to the scene of the fire. Yellow fingers of flame were already eating a patch of grass, creeping further and further, crackling and laying waste. Mandy swung the open can backwards, then sloshed it forward. Water hissed and beat back the orange menace. She swung again, from left to right. The flames danced for a moment, then died.

'Right, now throw the sheet over it!' Mrs Hope told James. She stood by with a long branch to beat the fire out once the sheet was down.

Mandy gulped in smoke as she stepped out of the way. It stung her eyes and made her cough. But they'd done it; the fire was under control and the monkeys were safe.

'Just think what would have happened if we hadn't been here!' James gasped angrily. 'That driver would never even have known what he'd done.' By now the car was well out of sight.

'Never mind; we *were* here.' Mrs Hope calmed them down. 'Are all the monkeys OK, Thomas?'

He stood in the middle of the road checking

them off as they ran for cover. 'Yes. They were scared, but none of them got hurt.'

Mandy drew breath and coughed again. She rubbed her eyes. 'What about the mother and baby?'

'Fine. Come and look.'

She went back to the nutmeg tree where he pointed into the branches. There, almost hidden by the leaves, the dust and the smoke, two frightened faces peered down. The baby clung on for dear life, while the mother chattered with fright.

'It's OK,' Mandy whispered. 'It's all over. Now go and join the others!'

The mother trembled and jumped jerkily higher up the branch. She wouldn't trust even the sound of Mandy's gentle voice. She would wait up there until all the humans had gone.

'Come on,' James said. 'We're scaring them. Let's go.'

So, sadly, they went and sat in the Land-rover to decide what to do next. There by the roadside was a patch of burned and scorched grass about five metres long; a reminder of the disaster that had been so narrowly avoided.

'It's still too soon to start the engine,' Emily Hope decided. 'And it's too hot to stay here in the car.' The shadows had moved round and left the Land-rover in the sun's full glare.

'*Hakuna matata*! No problem!' Thomas said easily, as if the car hadn't broken down, as if the fire had never happened. He made his suggestion as if it was simply time to rest for lunch and take things easy. 'My Uncle Jambiani lives on a farm near here. We can go and visit him!'

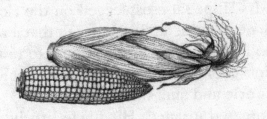

Three

'*Karibu, karibu*!' Thomas's uncle made them welcome and asked them to take off their shoes at the door. He spoke in Swahili to his nephew, while his pretty wife and small daughter stood by, smiling shyly.

From the outside, Mandy had noticed that the farmhouse was a simple square building made of mud, thatched with palm leaves. She expected the inside to be plain too, but she was pleasantly surprised by the shady hallway, carpeted with striped straw mats and hung with bright, patterned cloth. Uncle Jambiani led the group into the main room, where she found more mats, a low table and brass lamps fixed to the walls.

'My uncle says please will you eat with the family,' Thomas announced, as Mandy, James and Mrs Hope sat cross-legged on the floor.

'Oh no, thanks!' Emily Hope felt that it would be too much trouble. 'We just want to rest and wait in a cool place. We really don't want to put your uncle and aunt out.'

Thomas translated. His uncle brushed the protest aside.

'Uncle says my aunt would be very hurt if you didn't eat.'

Mandy listened to the flow of conversation as she gazed round the room. Through the open window she could see rows of beans and maize growing in rich red earth which sloped gently towards the skirts of the Mtondoo Forest. There the trees grew thick and shady, until they gave way to the bare, rocky peak of the mountain itself.

Very soon Mandy's mum gave in; they would eat at the farm. Thomas's uncle went off, beaming with pleasure.

'This is better!' James leaned against the cool wall. 'And with a bit of luck, the car will start after lunch and then we'll soon get close to where the monkeys live.'

'Will we have to leave the Land-rover and walk

into the forest?' Mandy asked Thomas. She had a picture of their small group stepping into the dark shadows of the trees, hacking a path through the jungle, like explorers of old.

Thomas nodded.

'What animals will we see besides monkeys?'

'Squirrels.'

Mandy tried not to look disappointed. Squirrels were clever, graceful little animals, but not exotic enough for Kima Punju. Not when she was dreaming of seeing a leopard.

'Gazelles, duikers, civets, snakes.' Thomas rattled them off.

She took a deep breath. 'Leopards?'

He shrugged. 'Maybe. Maybe not. A leopard is hard to see because of his spots.'

'And because he hunts at night, doesn't he?' Mrs Hope said. 'Do the farmers round here lose any of their cattle to the leopards?'

Thomas's uncle answered for him as he came in with the first of the dishes for lunch. It was a plate of samosas and savoury doughnuts, freshly cooked. 'Not to the leopard,' he said in slow, shaky English. 'The big cat hunts gazelles in the forest. He has no need to steal from the farms.' Then he spoke rapidly to his nephew in Swahili.

'What did he say?' Mandy asked.

'That the leopards hunt cane rats which eat the grass and sugar cane. He says the leopard is a friend of the farmer.'

Thomas's uncle spoke again. Mandy caught one or two words; '*Kima* . . . *Kima Punju*.' 'Is he talking about the monkeys now?' she asked.

Thomas nodded and shuffled his feet. 'He says the only animal from the forest he hates is the Poison Monkey.'

She bit her lip and stared at the tall, gentle man as he left for the kitchen and came back with another dish, this time of fish grilled over an open fire. It smelled smoky and delicious, served with salad and spicy vegetables. 'He doesn't still believe those old stories, does he?'

Thomas gave another one of his shrugs. His mouth was full of fish, picked from the dish with his fingers. He told the others to follow his lead.

Mandy glanced at her mum. Emily Hope was giving her a warning look. Mandy knew what it meant and stopped asking questions. Of course it would be rude to criticise Uncle Jambiani. But on the other hand, Mandy was worried about the monkeys. Last night, when Soud had told them the old legend, she'd been able to brush it aside as silly superstition. Now though, it seemed that the farmers really *did* have a thing against the monkeys.

They ate as much as their stomachs could hold: course after course of vegetables, fish, then fruit. When they'd finished, Emily Hope asked to go to the kitchen where she wanted to thank Jambiani's wife, Manyara. Meanwhile, Thomas gestured at James and Mandy to come outside.

'I can hardly move!' James groaned, his hands across his stomach.

'I want to show you something.' Thomas led them round the back of the house, between the tall rows of maize. It grew higher than their heads; each plant had a thick, straight stem and a sheath of green leaves protecting the head of corn. 'Uncle Jambiani grows the maize to sell in the market. My Aunt Manyara also has a stall by the side of the road. She cooks the maize in an oven which she makes out of fire and earth, then she sells it for a few shillings to travellers who pass by. This is how they live.'

Mandy and James understood that the farmers didn't make much money and must find it hard to feed and clothe their families. But they wondered why Thomas was taking such trouble to explain. He led them to the edge of the field, where his uncle had planted a more recent crop. Here the maize was only waist high, and the corn heads hardly formed.

Mandy looked more closely before she took Thomas's point. 'Something's been nibbling them!' She saw teeth marks in the tender shoots.

'And here.' James agreed that the damage was bad. 'These plants will die now, won't they?'

'Yes. And the crop can't be harvested, so there'll be no maize to take to market or sell at the roadside.' For once, Thomas didn't smile.

'Are you saying it's the monkeys?' Mandy asked, not wanting to accept the evidence before her own eyes. 'Couldn't it be something else?'

Thomas shook his head. 'Don't you believe monkeys would do this? Do you want to see it for yourself?' He walked on, skirting the field of maize until they came to a small orchard of lemon trees. Then he warned them to stop. He pointed to the figure of a boy sitting motionless under one of the trees. 'Watch!'

Mandy felt the sun on her back. She could smell the sweet blossom of the lemon trees, hear the cicadas scratching out their loud, buzzing chorus. In the distance, a heat haze shimmered over the mountain.

'Who's that?' James whispered. The boy was dressed in a white shirt and dark blue shorts. He squatted under the tree, holding a stout stick in one hand.

'That's my cousin, Jozani.'

A trickle of sweat crept down Mandy's forehead. 'What's he doing?' It seemed that the boy would never move, that he was a crouching statue.

Then they saw movement in the spiky bushes beyond the trees. A big group of animals came trotting towards the orchard; there were flashes of red-brown fur, black faces, long tails in the fawn grass. More than twenty of them came rustling towards the lemon trees.

'Uh-oh!' James muttered.

'Shh!' Thomas warned. Still Jozani didn't move a muscle.

It was the monkeys, of course. They came scampering and running, rolling and tumbling between the gnarled tree-trunks, swinging up into the branches and reaching out to take the youngest, tenderest leaves from the tips. White blossom fell to the ground as they climbed, showering on to Jozani's dark head. Then, at exactly the right moment, before the monkeys had settled to feed, he sprang up.

He rattled the stick against the trunks, running and shouting, waving the stick above his head. Mandy jumped with fright.

'*Yow-yow-yow!*' The monkeys took off. They swung through the trees, away from the rattling stick, grasping the branches and retreating from the orchard before they could eat the tender leaves and unripe fruit. '*Yow-yow-yow!*' They howled their disgust at being denied their lunch.

As soon as the coast was clear, Thomas took James and Mandy to meet his cousin. Jozani was shy, like his mother and sister; a boy of about

ten, whose stick was taller than he was. His grin showed rows of crooked teeth. '*Jambo*.' He seemed to stare at Mandy's blonde hair and James's glasses.

'Does he sit here and scare the monkeys all day?' Mandy asked. By now, there was no sign of them. They'd run shrieking back into the forest.

'No. In the morning he goes to school. My uncle can't be here all the time either; he has to work in the fields. So the monkeys eat the leaves and fruit of the lemon trees when they can. Uncle Jambiani gets angry and curses them. If he could, he would kill them.'

Thomas's answer was calm and matter-of-fact. But Mandy gasped. 'Kill them? You don't mean it!'

'Why not?' Thomas spread the palms of his hands upwards. 'Yes, sure; he would kill them without thinking. You must understand; all the farmers on the island hate the monkeys. To people like you, the monkey may be a sweet thing, a kind of pet. But to the farmers, the *kima* is a big, big problem!'

Four

'Poor monkeys!' Mandy sighed as soon as they got on the road again and left the farm behind. She'd tried hard to see the farmers' point of view, but still her stomach turned at the idea that they wanted to kill the monkeys like pests.

'Just a minute; let me listen to this engine!' Mrs Hope craned forward. 'It sounds OK again. Now, what were you saying, Mandy?'

'She's feeling sorry for the monkeys,' James told her, as Mandy stared through the window at the forest where they lived.

'You have to try to understand,' Emily Hope told her. 'It's like foxes back in England. *You* may think they're beautiful, but a lot of farmers don't. Maybe you wouldn't either, if they sneaked into your hen coop and stole your chickens.'

'I would!' Mandy claimed. 'I'd just build better hen coops to keep the foxes out. I definitely wouldn't kill them.'

'It does seem a bit unfair.' James took Mandy's side. 'The monkeys can't win on this island.'

'How do you mean?' Mrs Hope swung the Land-rover to the left to avoid a deep hole. They all swayed and clung on.

'Well, no one seems to look after them. On the one hand, the farmers go after them and try to get them because of their crops. On the other, tourists can harm them because they're careless, like that driver we saw today.'

Mandy sighed. 'I bet a lot of them die through tourists giving them the wrong food as well.'

'It's a wonder there are any left at all,' James agreed gloomily.

'Oh, come on, it's not that bad!' Mandy's mum put her foot on the brake. They'd come to the end of the track. Up ahead, a canopy of trees cut out the sun. 'Tell Mandy and James not to worry so much, Thomas. These monkeys have been here for thousands of years. I'm sure they can look after themselves, can't they?'

As they parked and jumped out of the Land-rover, reaching for their rucksacks and cameras, Thomas was slow to answer. He stood looking uncomfortable, waiting for them to get ready to set off on the walk into the forest.

'They can, can't they?' Mrs Hope repeated the question.

'That depends.' He looked away; down at his feet, along the track they would take, up at the cloudless sky.

'On what?' Mandy felt another jolt of alarm. She half-ran to catch up with him.

'On many things.' He walked on, still avoiding a direct answer.

'What are you saying? Are the monkeys in serious danger? How many of them are there left on Kima Punju?' she demanded.

'Nobody knows exactly. Ten years ago there were five thousand. Five years ago, there were only three thousand, so the government stopped felling the mahogany trees where they live, hoping that it would help.'

'Are their numbers still dropping?' They'd entered the shadow of ancient trees that spread overhead like giant umbrellas. Their fat trunks were reddish-brown, covered with creepers. Palms and ferns grew at their feet.

Thomas nodded. 'Three years ago they

counted eight hundred of them.'

'Eight hundred?' Mandy gasped in horror. 'That's terrible!' And that was three years ago. How many could be left after another three years of farmers killing them and tourists spoiling their habitat? She stopped and looked up into the trees.

There, hiding in the leaves, clinging to the swaying branches were the remaining monkeys. She felt eyes staring down at her, imagined their suspicion as she set foot into their world. How many? Five hundred? Four hundred? Fewer?

'Come on, Mandy,' James urged. Mrs Hope had caught up with Thomas and walked ahead. 'You don't want to get left behind.'

She let her gaze drop to the ground. Great roots of the mahogany trees twisted and writhed like snakes across the track. The forest smelled of damp earth and darkness. For the first time in her life, she was frightened, not just for one animal, but for a whole species.

'What if they die out?' she whispered to James, refusing to move from the spot. 'What if, a few years from now there are no Poison Monkeys left in the whole wide world?'

The forest made Mandy shiver. Here the daylight had a green tinge, and gone were the golden rays, the intense heat of the coast and the farmland. As she trod the path behind Thomas, her mum and James, she half-expected a frightened duiker, the tiny African deer, to spring out of the undergrowth, fleeing from an enemy, or a snake to coil itself down from the branch of a tree, tongue flicking, eyes glittering.

But all she actually saw was a group of gazelles quietly nibbling the grass in a small clearing. Heads down, with their graceful, curved horns and delicate white legs, they looked calm and peaceful.

'Are you OK?' Mrs Hope waited. 'You seemed a bit upset back there.'

'I'm fine now.' Mandy put on a brave face, trying not to worry about the fate of the monkeys. After all, what could she do? The problem was too big for her. As one single person visiting Kima Punju for a week, she couldn't solve a whole wildlife crisis all by herself.

'Come on, let's catch up and ask Thomas if there's any sign of these leopards,' her mum suggested. 'Though since it's the middle of the afternoon, they're all likely to be curled up fast asleep somewhere.'

They walked on, past the grazing gazelles, under a tall eucalyptus tree and into the dense shadow of more mahogany trees. At every step Mandy flicked her gaze here and there, watching, listening for signs of life. *No monkeys*, she said to herself, still gripped with worry.

They walked on until a huge mahogany tree blocked their path. The track split in two and went to either side of the tree, but Thomas stopped the others and pointed to a crumbling wall and some rusting iron beams. 'This is where the tree fellers used to saw their logs,' he explained. 'It's the old saw mill. Now the forest is taking it back.'

Mandy saw it was true. Tall grass grew up through the bricks, mingled with bright orange and red flowers. There were the remains of an old lorry, minus its wheels, all battered and rusty. Startled, she pointed to a broad snout and a pair of fierce tusks that peered out from under the wreck.

'Warthog,' Thomas said, as the creature shot nimbly from his hiding-place, his little legs flashing by, his pointed tail sticking straight up.

James, who had disappeared to the far side of the giant tree, called them to follow. 'Come and look at this!'

Mandy thought he sounded different; his voice was strained and muffled. When she made her way over the twisted roots to join him, she followed the direction of his pointing finger.

'What do you suppose that is?' he whispered.

'What? I can't see anything.' She peered into the shadows.

'Up there in that bare tree!'

She looked again. The dead tree was like a dry grey skeleton, without a single leaf on its branches. It rose way above their heads, then forked into two. There was something lying in the fork. Mandy took a step back and put her hand to her mouth.

'What is it?' James took off his glasses and cleaned them on his T-shirt. 'Is it the body of some sort of animal?'

'It looks like it,' she whispered. There were stiff legs dangling, a head hanging. 'I think it's a deer.'

'Gazelle.' Thomas came up from behind. 'A leopard's kill, probably. The leopard drags the body into a tree, away from other greedy animals.'

'How did it get all the way up there?' James asked. The body was wedged into the fork about ten metres above ground.

'They're very strong, very clever.'

Mandy looked cautiously all around. 'Where is he now?'

'Sleeping in the bushes until dusk. Don't worry, he won't bother us. We probably won't even see him.'

'Just as well,' Emily Hope said, as she came to join them. 'A leopard will attack practically anything it comes across. Have you ever seen one kill its prey, Thomas?'

'Only once.' His eyes shone at the memory. 'Long ago, when I was a small boy. This leopard was a female. She crept into a tree and lay in wait, stretched out along a branch.' He copied the creeping movement of the animal as he told his story. 'She was beautiful; white on her belly, yellow on her back, with dark spots. When she was still, you couldn't tell which was leopard and which was tree.'

'Amazing!' Mandy breathed.

'Waiting and waiting until a herd of gazelles came by. She chose carefully; one not too big, not too strong. She waited until the young gazelle strayed beneath her branch. The gazelle munched the grass, the leopard froze above, waiting for her moment.' Thomas crouched. 'Then down in a mighty leap, claws out, dropping on to the back of the gazelle! She felled it and seized it by the throat, sinking her teeth into its neck. The gazelle never even knew what had happened.'

Mandy sighed, James stared up at the corpse of the gazelle in the bare fork.

'When it was dead, she took it between her jaws and dragged it to her tree. She climbed high, hid the body in the branches where nothing else could climb. Then she was happy.'

'Hmm.' Mrs Hope folded her arms. 'It makes me pretty glad that there are no hungry leopards around today.'

They decided to hurry on, just in case.

'Where does this track lead?' James asked, eager to stride ahead, clear of the shadows of the giant mahogany.

'To the mountain.' Thomas picked up a stick and beat back a bush that had grown over the path. 'There's something special for Mandy,' he promised. The smile was back on his face, there was a spring in his step.

'It had better be good,' James teased. 'I hope it'll cheer her up!'

'Wait and see.' Thomas pushed on along the narrow path.

'What is it?' The boys' teasing took Mandy's

mind off fierce leopards and vanishing monkeys. She glanced at her mum, who just shrugged and shook her head.

'A surprise.' Thomas strode ahead. 'A nice surprise.'

He led them steadily through the forest, along a winding track to Mtondoo Mountain.

Five

' *"Mtondoo Mountain Relocation Centre."* '

Mandy read the sign outside the small hut at the foot of the mountain. 'What does it mean?' she asked.

Thomas kept up his mysterious smile. They'd walked steadily uphill until they'd come to the far edge of the forest. Now he led them through the door into a shady room with a desk and a notice-board.

'Relocation means they're moving something somewhere, doesn't it?' James stood in the doorway, trying to work out why Thomas had brought them here. 'But the notice doesn't tell us what it is.'

Mrs Hope had wandered over to look at the notice-board. 'I think I'm just beginning to guess,' she said with a smile.

Mandy and James joined her and looked at the pictures.

' "The Kima Punju Red Colobus",' Emily Hope read out loud. ' "You are about to experience one of Africa's rarest primates, the Kima Punju Red Colobus. There are only seven hundred and fifty of these unique monkeys left in the world, and all are found in the Mtondoo Forest on the island of Kima Punju." '

'Look at these photographs!' Mandy exclaimed. The pictures showed monkeys sitting on branches and scrambling over rocks, monkeys grooming and eating, monkeys swinging through the trees.

' "One of the most striking features of the Kima Punju Red Colobus is a crown of long white hairs which fans out round the face in tufts." ' James took over from Mrs Hope, reading the information while she strolled back to wait with Thomas at the desk. 'Why are these notices here?' he asked. There were a lot of them, telling him what the monkeys ate, and where they lived.

' "To help conserve the Kima Punju Red

Colobus, please give generously to the donation box." ' Mandy read a sign below the photographs. 'That's it! I get it!' she grew excited and pulled James towards the desk. 'They're collecting money to help save the monkeys!'

'Quite right,' a deep voice said, and a small man came out from a back room. '*Jambo*, Thomas. *Shikamoo*? How are you?' He shook hands and smiled at his visitors.

'*Maharaba*. Good. *Jambo*, Luke.' Thomas returned the greeting, then he introduced Mandy, James and Mrs Hope to the official warden. 'Luke Pemba is in charge here,' he explained. 'He can tell Mandy the good news about the monkeys.'

'What would you like to know?' Mr Pemba folded his arms. He was a short man, strongly built, dressed in a white shirt and jeans, wearing a big silver watch.

'Is this a rescue centre?' Mandy stared round the small office. 'Are you trying to help the monkeys by moving them out of danger?'

He nodded. 'Right again. The government employs me to see that the monkeys are legally protected. But their numbers are still falling, I'm afraid.'

'And what will you do?' Here at last was

someone who felt the same way as she did about the poor monkeys. She liked Luke Pemba the moment she saw him and heard his cheerful, friendly voice.

'Move them,' he said simply. 'That's what our relocation scheme is all about. If the monkeys can't survive on this side of the mountain, where there are too many farmers and too many tourists, we must move them to the other side, so they can live in peace.'

'Wow!' James was impressed. 'Are you going to move all of them?'

'Yes, all seven hundred and fifty. Here, on the west of the island, they can't live happily any longer. Much of the forest has gone, and so they come out of the trees to raid food from the farms. The monkeys are at war with the farmers. But on the east side of the island, the land is hilly. There are no farms, but plenty of almond trees, figs, coconut and mango. Plenty of food for monkeys!'

'But what about the tourists?' James objected. 'Won't they still bother the monkeys?' He told Mr Pemba about the man in the Land-rover earlier that morning.

'Hmm.' He frowned. 'Our visitors to the island mean well, but they can be careless. Sometimes they ignore the rules. What can we do?'

'Does it happen often?' James asked.

Luke Pemba shrugged. 'Let's just say it's one of the reasons why we must find a new home for the monkeys.' He turned back to Mandy. 'So, this is the good news: soon the monkeys will have a new place to live, away from the roads and the farmland. They will settle into the forest again, their numbers will increase, the species will survive.'

She smiled back at him. 'How soon is soon?'

'By the end of this month the relocation scheme will be complete and I will be out of a job!'

'That *is* quick!' she gasped. 'Does that mean you've moved some of the monkeys already?'

'More than five hundred. That's why, if you've been looking for them as you walked along the forest trail, you might not have seen them. Many have already been moved to the east of the island.'

'So that's why!' Mandy was relieved to discover the reason. 'I expected there to be lots, but we only saw the ones on Thomas's uncle's farm.'

'We did see the remains of a leopard kill,' James added. 'And a warthog, at the old sawmill.'

'But no monkeys?' Mr Pemba reached for his cap hanging on a hook behind the desk. 'Would you like to see some now?'

'Do fish swim in the sea?' Mrs Hope said with a smile.

Mandy and James had already raced to the door.

'*Kek-kek-kek*!' A male monkey chattered a warning as Luke Pemba led them back into the forest. The monkey was hidden in the trees, but the warden explained to Mandy and James what the sound meant.

'He's telling you that this is his territory: Keep out. Now, you hear that noise?'

Mandy listened. She heard '*Eek-eek*!' from the undergrowth. 'Yes, what's that?' She flicked an insect from her face, then stared into the bush.

'That's a female. We've caught her off-guard. It's the sound she makes when she's surprised.'

'I still can't see her.' Mandy had the same feeling as earlier; that the forest was full of eyes watching them as they walked. The shadows swayed and shifted, sunlight danced on a patch of open land, then the trees closed over them again. 'They must be really good at hiding!'

'Be patient. Wait until they've got used to us, then they'll come out to feed.' Mr Pemba motioned for them to stop in a small clearing, where bright blue birds swooped to catch flies.

'A family troop comes here to feed in the afternoon,' he explained. 'One old male, three females and five young ones. We call them the Black Plum family because they feed mainly from this tree here.' He pointed to a fruit tree dripping with small deep purple fruit.

'Will you be moving these monkeys soon?' James asked. He stood in a patch of sun, squinting up at the tree.

Luke nodded. 'As soon as we can.'

'*Ooo-ooo!*' Leaves rustled in the mahogany tree behind them as they turned to look. '*Ooo-ooo-ooo!*'

'That's a young one. He sounds hungry,' Thomas told Mandy. 'It shouldn't be long now.'

'You seem to know a lot about them,' she said slowly, looking impatiently from branch to branch. 'How come?'

'Didn't he tell you?' The warden overheard and gave a tut. 'Typical Thomas. He's a very modest boy. The truth is, when he's at home on Kima Punju, Thomas is one of my best unpaid helpers. When he's away working on safari, I miss him very much!'

Thomas looked at the ground and shuffled. Mandy and James stared.

'Yes, yes. Every day he cycles from town and leaves his bike at Jambiani's place. Then he joins me at the Centre to help with the monkeys. He knows every family by name; the Black Plums and the Coconut Palms, the Mangoes and the Limes. When the time comes to move a family across the mountain, there he is, ready to help. How many families have you helped me with now, Thomas? It must be six or seven. That would be nearly eighty monkeys in all.'

'Eighty!' Mandy saw Thomas in a new light. She'd always liked him, ever since they'd arrived in Africa. He was bright and cheerful, even at six in the morning, going about his jobs at camp with lots of energy and enthusiasm. He cooked a supper of rice and vegetables over the campfire in big, steaming metal pans. The food was always delicious. But she'd never realised before now that he was interested in animals. 'You never said anything!' she hissed.

'You never asked,' he replied calmly.

'Shh!' James warned. The ooo-oooing was growing louder. Hunger was driving the young monkeys into the open. Two of them appeared on a branch of the mahogany tree and peered down suspiciously.

'Here they come,' Thomas whispered.

Deciding it was safe, they swung from the branch to a hanging creeper, carefully making their way around the clearing to the tempting plum tree. Their feet didn't touch the ground as they swayed like gymnasts from creeper to creeper, until they perched high in the fruit tree and began to pick the plums neatly one at a time between their nimble fingers.

'Aren't they gorgeous?' Mandy breathed. Their silky fur shone rusty red in the sunlight, the white ruffs around their faces made them look like clowns. And now their cheeks puffed out as they stuffed them full of fruit, stopping every so often to spit out the stones with a sharp smack of their lips.

'*Wah-wah!*' One of the monkeys cried out with pleasure, bringing others following him into the clearing.

Mandy watched as three fully grown adults came into view. There was a whoosh and a rustle of leaves as they came swinging strongly through the trees, passing to either side of the group of intruders. One was so close that she

could almost have reached out to touch its soft
back. Its tail swished against her, then it was
gone, hidden in the branches of the plum tree.

'And here comes Grandma!' Luke murmured.

Mandy turned to watch a wizened old monkey
come slowly into the clearing. She walked on all
fours, head up, deciding to ignore the bunch of
strangers who'd invaded her afternoon feeding
place. Her fringe of white hair was long and
bushy, her stiff legs were pale grey, and as she
picked fallen plums from the ground, she moved
her jaws slowly sideways, sighing contentedly.

'She looks like an old lady without any teeth!'
Mandy whispered, her blue eyes sparkling. 'Oh
look, what are those two up to?'

The two young monkeys had scrambled down
the tree towards the grandma. For a moment,
Mandy thought they were going to steal her food,
but then they started to play on the ground
nearby, tumbling and somersaulting, knocking
into her as they rolled and wrestled.

Quick as a flash, the old lady let fly with her
hand. Whack! She caught them each a blow on
the side of the head. '*Yow-yow*!' they cried.

'Ouch!' Mandy smiled. The old lady wasn't
so slow and stiff after all. The two youngsters

pushed out their bottom lips like sulky children.

'That'll keep them quiet,' Mrs Hope said.

The naughty monkeys crouched at Grandma's side, reaching out to pick at her ruff of white fur, grooming her and telling her they were sorry.

'They're just like humans!' Mandy decided.

'That female is seventeen years old,' Luke told them. 'And the others know she's the boss round here.'

'And you say they come here every day? They must be highly territorial,' Emily Hope remarked.

Luke agreed. 'They have well-marked sleeping, feeding and sunning places, with connecting routes in between. That's what makes it so difficult to move them.'

'So what do you do?' Mandy wanted to know. The longer she watched, the more fascinating she found these creatures. She stared at an adult male in the tree, as he smacked his lips, then spat out a volley of plum stones.

'We look for a similar home for them on the other side of the mountain. When we find a group of black plum trees for this family, we'll put the monkeys in cages, trek them across to their new area and set them free again.'

Mandy listened carefully. 'One family at a time?'

'Yes. Each group needs about half a square kilometre. We wait for them to mark out their territory, then we begin again with the next family. And so on. That's why the relocation scheme is taking a long time. Remember, there are no roads to the east, so we must go by foot. It depends on volunteers.'

She nodded, still searching for more monkeys. 'Didn't you say there were some babies in this family?' She looked around in vain.

'Up there.' Thomas pointed to a low branch

of a mahogany tree, to where a pair of mothers sat quietly with their young ones. 'They're just about ready to come and feed.'

He was right. The females came cautiously to join the others, checking that the humans meant them no harm. Mandy looked hard. The babies' faces peeped out at her, their dark eyes staring. One clung tightly to his mother's belly, but the other was so tiny that the mother had to cradle him gently in one arm as she loped along.

'Oh!' Mandy cried out in delight.

The two mothers turned sharply, then edged away.

'Let's leave them in peace,' Luke suggested, showing the way out of the clearing without making more noise.

Mandy gazed on. The Black Plum family was complete; young and old together. She watched as the babies suckled noisily and the lively youngsters played another game. She smiled at the grandma spitting out stones one by one.

'Come on, Mandy.' Mrs Hope tugged her gently by the arm. 'Maybe we can come back another day.'

'What was that?' Luke Pemba stopped and waited for them to catch up. 'Did I hear someone offer to help?' he called.

Mandy gasped and blushed. It was as if Luke Pemba could read her mind. She looked from James to Thomas, to her mum. There was a long pause.

'Or was I mistaken?' Luke teased. 'Never mind. It was only that I was thinking of moving the Black Plum family across the mountain as soon as I can find some volunteers to help.' He turned to walk on, back to the office.

'What do you say?' Mandy urged. 'Shall we?'

'Shall we what?' James grinned. He swivelled his cap round back-to-front and stuck both hands in his pockets.

'You know!'

'No, I don't. Shall we what?'

Mandy was so excited she felt she would burst. 'Shall we volunteer? We could come back tomorrow and help Luke move the whole family! That would be amazing, wouldn't it? To be part of saving a whole species!'

She was fired up, ready to run and tell Luke he could rely on them. She would do anything; get up before dawn, climb a mountain! 'Oh, what do you say?' she begged.

'Just try and stop me,' James replied, racing on ahead.

Six

Back in town late that afternoon, Mandy flew up the steps at Thomas's house ahead of Thomas, James and her mum. She took the stairs two at a time to the room where her parents were staying.

'Dad!' She knocked on the door. 'Are you in there? We've had an amazing day. I've got something to ask you!'

There was no reply, so she shot up more stairs on to the roof terrace and called again.

Thomas's father, Soud, was there, taking it easy. He sat looking out at the harbour, watching the *dhows* sail by. The boats had colourful sails, deep red and blue, as well as white, and they criss-crossed the water at a steady pace, bobbing on the waves.

Soud turned and smiled. '*Jambo*, Mandy. If you want your father, you'll find him on the beach.'

'You mean, he's still there?' She pictured him frazzled by the sun after a whole day in the sun, while they went on their tour to see the monkeys on the mountain.

'No. He's been home for lunch, had a long siesta and now he's gone back to watch the sunset. Your father's a man who knows how to relax.'

'He sure is.' Mandy was already on her way downstairs again. She bumped into her mum on the way up. 'Dad's gone back to the beach. Can I go and look?'

Emily Hope nodded. 'But remember, your father's enjoying taking time off from work. Don't expect him to be as excited as you are about the plight of the monkeys.'

Mandy had reached the front door, with its zigzag carvings and brass studs. She looked up and nodded. 'It's OK, Mum. I'll make sure I tell him he doesn't have to join in with us tomorrow if he doesn't want to!' She was overjoyed that her mother had said yes to Luke Pemba's request for help. It would be great if her dad would join in too – the whole family together – but she knew that he loved to sit and watch the world go by when he got the chance; after all, this *was* meant to be a holiday.

She ducked into the narrow, shady street, weaving between the children playing games. Women came in and out of the shops, some wearing veils across their faces, while the men sat at their doors, hunched over a game of *Bao*, played on a wooden board with dozens of small balls which they scooped up and dropped into rows of empty dishes. They glanced up as Mandy ran by, heading for the harbour and the beach beyond.

She noticed a big white ferry steering into port, carrying its cargo of tourists and towns-people. Behind it, the golden sun sank towards the water. Close by, the harbourside was almost empty. A row of *dhows* were moored, ready for the morning trips out to sea, but now most of the fishermen were at home with their families for the evening. Mandy ran on, eyes peeled, searching for her father.

The town beach stretched north of the harbour towards some ancient ruins, a long strip of white sand fringed by palm trees. From a distance it looked empty, but Mandy ran on, longing to tell her dad the news about the monkeys. Perhaps he was sitting in the shade of one of the trees by the old palace. As she stepped on to the sand, she stopped to kick off her shoes and carry them. She decided it would be quicker to paddle in the shallow water and make her way up to the ruins. If she didn't find him there, she would have to turn back and wait until he showed up for supper.

And that was the way it seemed to be turning out, as Mandy drew level with the crumbling building; once a splendid house with a domed roof and narrow, arched windows, but now empty and standing in ruins. *It looks like Dad must have cut back through the town*, she said to herself. The beach came to an end in a curve of sharp rocks. There was nothing for it but to give up and go home.

But a sound inside the ruined house caught her attention. She frowned, went towards it, and changed her mind. *No*, she thought, *if that was Dad, he'd have seen me coming. He wouldn't be hiding in that old place . . . Would he?*

Mandy stopped. There was the noise again, like small stones crumbling from the walls and dropping to the ground. It came from high up in the ruin, where branches of trees had grown up through the windows and roof. 'Dad?' She turned again and set foot on the chipped and broken stone steps leading up from the beach. She felt the sun on her back and paused again. The house was dark and shadowy. 'Is that you?' she called. Her voice echoed back.

It would be just like him to be playing a trick. More loose stones peppered down. 'Dad, this isn't funny!'

She heard someone in there. Feet ran away as she went up the steps. She caught a glimpse of bright blue and yellow as a figure vanished behind an inner doorway.

Mandy followed quickly, ignoring a fresh shower of stones from above. *This is hide-and-seek, then*, she told herself. *Trust you, Dad!*

She went through the door into another ruined room, with bushes growing from crevices in the walls and a tree pushing up through the floor. Empty! She tutted and climbed back out of the building through a low window. 'OK, Dad!' she cried, glad to be out in the fresh air. 'I give in. It's time for supper!'

If this didn't bring him out, nothing would, she thought.

A face looked out at her from another window, then a second face, then a third. All three were wide-eyed and smiling. They peeped and grinned, then climbed out to join her; a boy in a yellow T-shirt and shorts, a girl of about eight in a faded pink dress, and a tiny girl dressed in bright yellow and blue, with ribbons in her hair.

Mandy gasped, then grinned back in relief. 'Where did you come from?'

The older girl answered in a rush of Swahili. She pointed to a row of small houses up a track behind the ruins.

Mandy realised they must be fishermen's huts, from the nets set out to dry. She imagined how the children must have spied on her as she walked up the beach, then played their trick to tempt her into the old building. The little girl clung to the older girl's skirt, half-hiding, but peeking out with a mischievous smile. Mandy crouched down to her level. 'I'm Mandy,' she told her. 'What's your name?'

'Whass-your-name?' The boy echoed her words. 'Whass-your-name? Whass-your-name?' He was practising his English.

'Mandy,' she repeated. But she was puzzled. If these three had been the ones playing hide-and-seek, who had been throwing the stones? She glanced up at the ruined roof.

To her surprise, when she looked back at the

children, they were running away.

'Wait! What's wrong?' Their smiling faces were gone, and now they were dashing off towards the huts, the little one trailing behind. Had something scared them? Mandy looked up again and saw straight away what it must be.

Monkeys. There were two of them gazing down at her from the roof, picking up loose stones and throwing them to the ground. They ran here and there, jumping easily across broken sections, setting up a chattering cry as the three children ran and Mandy stopped to stare.

She wanted to call after the children, 'Don't be frightened. They won't harm you!' But she knew they wouldn't understand her words. In any case, the fishermen would know the old stories about the monkeys. Witch doctors and poison; all that nonsense. No wonder the kids were scared.

But what were the monkeys doing here, so far from the forest? Mandy looked up and shook her head. 'Are you lost?' she murmured. She hadn't heard of them straying to the beaches, though she knew they would leave the forest to raid the farms. Forgetting all about the three frightened children, she climbed back into the ruin to find out more.

Once inside, she remembered something that Thomas had told her about the monkeys. 'Don't stare straight at them,' he'd said. 'It scares them.' So she pretended not to take any notice of the two running along the beams and swinging through the overgrown branches as they followed her inside the house. She sat quietly on a fallen pillar, waiting for them to calm down. Sooner or later they would understand that she didn't mean to harm them. They would stop rattling stones down from their perch. Then she would try to find out what they were doing so far from home.

She waited for a few minutes, listening to the rush of waves on to the beach, watching the shadows lengthen. Gradually the monkeys grew calmer, coming down from the high ledges and boldly jumping on to the ground. They stared at Mandy with curious faces, still jittery and alert to every sound.

'Mandy!'

She heard James call her name. He sounded a long way off, at the far end of the beach. She didn't move or answer, frowning as the two monkeys shot back up on to the roof beams.

'Mandy, where are you?'

He was nearer this time, so she stood up and went to the door overlooking the sea. She waved and he came running up.

'Your dad's back at the house,' he explained. 'He arrived just after you left. He used a different route. You must have missed him.' He was breathless after his jog along the beach. 'I said I'd come and fetch you.'

'Thanks, James, but look what I've found!'

For the first time he gazed around him. 'Wow, what *is* this place?' He stared up at the flaking plaster, the ruined domes.

'It must be some kind of grand house, but never mind about that. Do you see those old beams in that far corner?' Mandy waited for him to spot the monkeys.

'Hey!' James skipped out of the way as a stone whizzed through the air. 'Who threw that?'

She pointed again. 'Behind that tall fig tree, on the beams, look!'

The monkeys chirped a high warning sound as James finally saw them. They swung out of sight, then reappeared. James was startled.

'Are you wondering the same as me?' Mandy asked.

'You mean, what they're doing here?'

She nodded. 'You know what, I think they're trying to show us something.' Until now she'd imagined they were anxious to hide, but could it be that the stone-throwing was meant to attract attention instead? After all, it was the noise they'd made that had drawn her over in the first place.

'What?' James turned full circle, looking high and low. 'Why would they do that?'

'I don't know. I just have this peculiar feeling.'

By this time the monkeys seemed to have accepted James and were busy chattering and chirping out another message. They'd gone back to the fig tree and started to do acrobatics again, swinging down towards the ground, then scampering up again between the broad leaves.

'Mandy, I think we ought to get back,' James said uneasily. 'I told them we wouldn't be long. Thomas said supper was nearly ready. They'll be expecting us.'

'OK, just a minute.' She walked quietly towards the tree, studied how it had taken root between cracks in the floor of the old building and grown up tall and strong. It branched out overhead, loaded with big green figs. 'There's something else up there,' she said slowly, craning her neck to see.

'*Yow-yow!*' The two monkeys raced up and down a branch, howling a warning.

Mandy reached up and tested the bottom branch, ready to climb. 'I'm going to take a look,' she told James.

He drew a sharp breath and glanced quickly round the shadowy building. 'OK, wait for me!'

She nodded. 'It looks easy enough, unless whatever it is that's up there decides to move when he sees us coming.' Mandy pulled herself up by her arms and straddled the bottom branch. Then she paused to look up again. 'No, he's not moving!'

James was trying a different route up the tree. 'Can you see what it is yet?'

'*Yow-yow-yow!*' The screeching grew louder, the monkeys jumped up and down with excitement.

'Not quite.' She heaved herself up another couple of feet. 'It's something lodged in the fork of that branch just above your head.' Mandy held on to the trunk and leaned sideways. Then she gasped. 'James, it's a monkey! It's only small. I don't think it's very well!'

He drew level, breathing hard. 'It's a young one,' he agreed.

The little monkey sat huddled up against the

trunk, his legs hunched up to his chin, shoulders up, head drooping. His long tail hung straight and still, and though he blinked at them and cowered away, he didn't try to move.

'He must be sick!' Mandy whispered. 'Otherwise he wouldn't let us get so close. And maybe the other two are his mother and father. They know how sick he is and they're asking us for help!'

James wasn't sure. 'I don't know about that.' He stepped out on to a branch to take a good look. 'But I do think he's poorly. I can see him shivering.'

'I wonder how long he's been here.' Suddenly things slotted into place. This explained why the monkeys hadn't gone back to the forest at the end of their day ranging about the island looking for food. The adults had stayed with the sick youngster, not knowing what to do. Then when the children had come in to play, they'd panicked. Now the stone-throwing and the angry cries all made sense.

'He's in a bad way, Mandy,' James muttered, edging even closer. 'He looks pretty weak. If we try to move him, the other two will think we're hurting him. But if we leave him here, I don't think he'll last long. What are we going to do?'

'We'll have to try and move him,' Mandy decided. 'If we can get him down, we can take him back to Thomas's house and Mum and Dad can have a look at him. It might be something they can treat.' She knew by his shivering and the dull look in his eyes that the young monkey might have some kind of fever. Or he could have food poisoning. In any case, her mum and dad would know.

'OK.' James agreed to try. 'Let me climb up and get him. It's easier from this side.'

Mandy watched as he slithered up on to the branch opposite the one where the sick monkey sat. Further up, the two adults shrieked and cried. If only she could explain. She hung on tight and held her breath as James sat astride the branch and reached out to grasp their patient.

It was done. There was a high chorus of screams and wails, but the monkey was safe in James's arms.

'Can you take him?' He reached down towards Mandy.

She nodded and took the monkey. She cuddled him close, feeling his little hands grasp at her hair as she eased herself down the tree, holding on to him at the same time. He was warm and silky soft, shaking with fear as they reached the ground and she clasped him with both arms.

But the crisis wasn't over. As James climbed down the tree and the grown-up monkeys swung wildly overhead, there were more voices, and feet running towards the ruin from the direction of the fishermen's huts. Mandy spied figures through the window. Four men waved their arms and shouted.

'Quick!' She backed off towards the door. 'We've got to get out of here!'

James landed beside her and saw what she meant. The fishermen shouted angrily and pointed up at the crumbling domes. '*Kima! Kima!*' They were armed with stones and sticks, their voices strained.

'Those kids must have gone back home and told their parents about the monkeys. Remember the old stories!' She knew that the sick baby monkey wouldn't stand a chance once the men spotted him. 'If they find us here, they'll kill him!' she gasped.

'Well, they haven't seen us yet!' James muttered. 'Let's get out of here before they do.' He hustled Mandy out of the door, down the broken steps on to the beach.

'What about the other two?' Mandy shuddered

as she heard the sound of large stones clattering against the walls of the building and the angry, disappointed cries of the men. She felt the young monkey grasp her tight and hide his head.

James shook his head. 'We'll just have to hope.'

She bit her lip. 'We can't leave them!'

'We have to, Mandy!'

The men had climbed through the windows with their long sticks. They rattled wildly at the fig tree and shook its branches. Up above, the two monkeys jumped through the ruined beams, out of reach. Luckily the men were so busy chasing them that they didn't turn to see James and Mandy on the beach with the baby.

'*Kima*! *Kima Punju*!' The cry went up again. The men believed that the monkeys would kill their trees and poison their animals. They would hound them out of their neighbourhood, or, worse still, kill them.

Mandy backed away in fright, cradling the young monkey in her arms. Then, when the waves lapped around her ankles, she came to her senses and realised there was only one choice. She nodded at James, turned away from the ruins and set off running with the monkey down the long white sands.

Seven

'Oh dear.' Adam Hope shook his head. He looked down at the small bundle of shivering fur as Mandy put the monkey down on her bed.

Her breath came in short gasps, her lungs hurt. 'Do something, Dad, please!'

James stood in the doorway, looking on. 'We didn't have any choice!' he told Mrs Hope. 'Honestly, he was so weak he couldn't even move. If we'd left him where he was, the fishermen would have killed him!'

She nodded and put a hand on his shoulder. 'OK, James, calm down. Let's just see if we can do anything for him before we worry about anything else.' She squeezed past him into

Mandy's bedroom. 'How does it look?' she asked.

'A bit grim.' Mandy's dad cupped his hand and stroked the monkey's head. 'He's very listless. That's probably partly the shock of recent events.'

'Try, Dad!' Mandy whispered. The poor little thing lay curled up. When Adam Hope lifted its hand then let go, its arm flopped back on to the bed.

'OK, Mandy, run to our room and fetch my first-aid kit. It's on the windowsill.'

Straightaway, she was out of the room and across the landing, grabbing the basic vets' bag that her mother and father took everywhere with them. Then she rushed back to where the monkey lay.

'Right, now open it and find a thermometer for me. My guess is that he's got some sort of fever, but I need to check.'

Mandy did as she was told. She was used to helping her parents at home at Animal Ark and didn't fumble or hesitate now. In fact, it felt better to be busy rather than standing by helpless.

'How's his pulse?' her mum asked.

'Fast and weak.' Mr Hope gently opened the

monkey's mouth and looked inside. 'He's lost fluid. I'd say he's pretty badly dehydrated, but we can soon put that right.' He took the thermometer from Mandy and took the monkey's temperature.

'Well?' Emily Hope stayed calm, forming her own opinion as Adam Hope worked.

'High. Definite fever. Mucus in the nose and the throat looks swollen.' He stood up to consider a verdict. 'You know what's wrong with this little chap?' he said, scratching his beard in a puzzled way.

'What?' Mandy couldn't bear the suspense. Was it something that could be cured, or not? The poor monkey lay shivering, with chattering teeth and snuffly nose.

'If I didn't know better, and if we weren't slap-bang on a tropical island within spitting distance of the Equator, I'd say he had common-or-garden flu!'

Mandy took a step forward and bent over the bed. 'Flu?' she whispered.

'Exactly. What would a monkey be doing catching flu on a paradise island?' Adam Hope said. 'People think it's a disease that people get if they live in a grotty cold climate, not an illness that you'd ever link with Africa.'

'Still, I think you may be right,' Emily Hope agreed. 'The symptoms fit. And it wouldn't be unheard of, you know, for an animal to catch a human virus. Flu can pass from species to species, I'm sure; especially to another primate.'

'Flu?' Mandy said again, stroking the monkey to comfort him. This didn't sound so bad. After all, people quickly recovered from flu. 'So what do we do now?'

Her dad still stood back stroking his beard. 'If we're right, there's no point giving him an antibiotic. And there's no effective vaccine against influenza once you've caught it.'

Mandy glanced up at the sound of his worried voice. 'He will get better though, won't he?'

Emily Hope stepped in briskly as Mandy's dad frowned. 'We'll do our best. First of all, Mandy, I want you to help me mix a glucose solution for him. He's too weak to drink, so we'll have to give it through a tube. We've done this lots of times in the surgery, and it's no different here, except that we must be especially careful to keep things sterile because of the heat. OK?'

'What will the glucose do?' James asked, as more activity began around him.

'Well, the fluid is to stop the dehydration, and the glucose will boost his sugar level,' Adam

Hope explained. 'We have to go very gently because he's so small and weak, but once we've done this, our main job will be to keep him warm. After that, it's a case of keeping a very careful eye on him and getting him to take liquid as often as possible. The water will have to be boiled and purified. That's a job you could do, James.'

It was time for Emily Hope to insert the plastic tube into the monkey's throat. Mandy stood by in case he put up a struggle. 'Easy does it,' Mrs Hope murmured. Then she gently pushed the tube all the way into the stomach, ready to begin trickling in the glucose mixture through a funnel on the end of the tube. 'In a while we'll see if we can add soluble aspirin to help take down the temperature.' She poured with a steady hand.

Soon they'd done all they could, so Mandy helped to clear away. 'Should we wrap him in something to keep him warm?' she asked. 'He'll need to sleep now, won't he?'

'Yes, plenty of peace and quiet,' her dad said. 'And fingers crossed, he should start to improve by morning.'

'You hear that?' Mandy whispered, as she tucked a sheet around the curled-up little body.

'My dad's a very good vet, so he knows what he's talking about! And he says you should be getting better soon!' She stroked him once more.

The monkey turned his head to look at her. He blinked and sighed.

'Poor little thing; I wonder what happened to your mum and dad,' she said softly. The wild cries of the angry fishermen as they chased the monkeys from the ruins rang in her head once more. 'I hope they got away!'

'Leave him to sleep.' Emily Hope took her by the hand. 'Come back in half an hour and check on him, after you've eaten your supper.'

'I'm not very hungry,' Mandy confessed.

'No, but you should eat.'

'Can I give him a name, Mum?' She tiptoed towards the door, gazing over her shoulder at the sick baby.

'Of course. We have to call him something. What shall it be?'

'Just Kima,' she said softly, her hand resting on the door handle. She lingered to give him one last look. 'Something plain and simple. Little Kima, sleep well,' she sighed. She went out and quietly closed the door.

*

'One of the rules Luke has is "Please do not visit the monkeys if you have any illness, especially a cold or flu." ' Thomas explained the reason to Mandy as she sat picking at the food on her plate. 'It's because people are the main threat to the monkey. We can definitely pass on human diseases to them, and their bodies can't fight back the way ours can.'

'So I wonder who went too near Kima.' Mandy lifted a forkful of rice, but her hand stopped partway to her mouth.

'Someone who didn't know the rules, obviously.' James sat frowning across the table from Mandy.

She scraped her chair back and stood up. 'I'll just go and check he's OK,' she said quietly.

But Emily Hope reached out and stopped her. 'Not yet, Mandy. Let him sleep. We really have done all we can for now.' She smiled kindly. 'I know what it's like, believe me. But try and be patient. Sleep is often the best healer, and the worst thing you could do is disturb him.'

'What worries me is what happened to the mum and dad,' James said. 'Those fishermen looked pretty angry.'

'What would they do if they caught the

monkeys?' Adam Hope asked Soud. The two men stood on the terrace, looking out at the starlight reflected on the shimmering black waves.

'They look on them as pests.' Soud stared out to sea, unable to reassure them.

Mandy sat down and gazed at her lap. If only the three children hadn't come to the ruins to play their game of hide-and-seek. If only they hadn't run and told the grown-ups. She pictured a happy ending for Kima: he would get better from his dose of flu, she and James would feed him up and take him back to the ruined house. His mum and dad would be perched in the fig tree waiting for him. They would greet him and take him back to the Mtondoo Forest. The family would be together again.

Now, because of the angry fishermen, none of that was possible.

'Have we had any news?' Adam Hope went on. 'You know, any actual account of what happened to the adults?'

Soud shook his head. 'But remember, to the people of the island, the monkeys aren't important. Sure, they chase them away. They even kill them. But to them it's normal, like you would kill a fly in England.'

'I wouldn't even kill a fly,' Mandy said, too worried to think about being polite.

'Yes, *you* might not. But I see what Mr Nungwi means,' her mother pointed out. 'At home, if someone swatted a fly, they wouldn't bother to advertise it or shout it from the roof-tops. The same with monkeys here.'

'We'll just have to wait and see,' Mr Hope said. 'And concentrate on looking after Kima. OK?'

When at last Mandy was allowed back to her room to check on the sick monkey, Kima was sleeping soundly.

'That's a good sign,' Adam Hope said quietly. 'Feel his forehead, though. He's still very hot.'

Mandy stroked Kima's head. 'That means he's still feverish.'

'Yes, but fighting back. The thing is, he's dehydrating very quickly because of the fever, so it's time to wake him up to give him water.' Mr Hope turned to James. 'Did you bring that boiled water up from the kitchen?'

James handed him a metal flask. 'Has it cooled down enough?'

'Yes, it's fine. Now, we shouldn't need a stomach tube this time. With a bit of luck, Kima will be stronger after his sleep. He should be able to take the water from a syringe.' Mr Hope reached into his bag.

'No need,' Mandy said quickly. She showed her dad a baby's feeding bottle. 'James and I went into the town to the chemist's while you were drinking your coffee. We thought Kima would like this better.'

Her dad grinned. 'Good thinking.'

'And we sterilised it,' James said earnestly. 'Thomas's mum helped us while we were boiling the water in the kitchen.'

'Well, that's great.' Mr Hope poured the water into the bottle with a steady hand. 'Now, Mandy, you can wake Kima up. Keep him wrapped in the sheet to keep warm. Have you got him safe? OK, now try him with the water. That's it, gently does it.'

She took the baby monkey and cradled him in one arm. With her other hand, she offered him the bottle. He blinked sleepily up at her. 'At least you're not shivering any more,' she whispered. 'Come on, drink this. It'll do you good.'

She nuzzled the bottle to his lips and at last he opened his mouth and began to suck. Soon the water was all gone.

'More?' James suggested.

'No, not just now. But, James, you can put this plastic cover on top of a pillow, put the whole thing in the wooden orange box that Soud gave us and make a bed for Kima in the corner of the room. Put more pillows around it as a kind of fence, so he won't fall out. That's good. Now, Mandy, when you've finished there, you can snuggle him down over here.' Adam Hope was brisk. 'The sooner we can get him off to sleep again, the better.'

Kima was warm and comfortable in her arms. Reluctantly Mandy followed her father's advice. 'You be good,' she whispered down at him as she made him cosy in the specially made bed.

'Sleep well. In the morning you'll feel much, much better!'

He blinked, then closed his eyes. Within seconds he was fast asleep.

'What do you think?' James asked, as he and Mr Hope began to tiptoe out of the room. It was time for everyone to get some rest. 'Is he going to be all right?'

Mandy's dad showed them his crossed fingers. 'Time will tell. Make sure you sleep properly,' he warned her. 'Remember you have to be up and off in good time tomorrow, to help at the relocation centre.'

Startled, she looked up.

'You hadn't forgotten, had you?'

'No. Well, yes, kind of . . .' Mandy was flustered. 'No, it's OK, I remembered!'

Her dad looked hard at her. 'You did volunteer to help tomorrow and I expect Luke Pemba is relying on you.'

'I'll be there,' she insisted. But how could she leave Kima for a whole day, knowing how ill he was? How could she even get a wink of sleep?

'Good girl.' The door was almost shut behind him as her dad put his head back in the room. 'Because a promise is a promise, you know.'

Eight

Mandy went straight to bed, but she found it hard to sleep. Every cough and snuffle from Kima got her out of bed and padding barefoot across the cool, tiled floor to peek into his box. Half a dozen times she sneaked a look; whenever he sneezed, or once because she'd lain awake listening and feared that he was too quiet. She breathed a sigh of relief when she saw that he was sleeping soundly.

He woke up three times during the night to drink, taking water eagerly from the bottle, reaching up with his little black hands to tilt it into his mouth. After the last time, at four o'clock in the morning, Mandy had put him back to bed and at last managed to get some sleep herself.

'How's the patient?' Adam Hope knocked and came into her room as the dawn light filtered through the shutters.

Mandy groaned and opened one eye. Then in a flash she remembered everything and jumped out of bed. Her eyelids pricked from lack of sleep, the whole room seemed fuzzy, but she tiptoed to the corner. 'He's still sleeping,' she reported. 'Come in and see what you think, Dad.'

He joined her, yawning, and crouched down by the box. 'I thought I'd nip in and take his temperature,' he explained.

'Couldn't you sleep either?'

'Not much. How about you?'

'Nope. What's it say?'

Adam Hope read the thermometer. 'It's well down, nearly back to normal.'

Mandy drew a deep breath. 'He's had plenty to drink. That's good, isn't it?'

He nodded then tucked Kima up again. 'Like any young mammal, if they get sick they go down pretty quickly unless they get treatment, but once they're on the mend, they come up quickly too.' He stood up and put an arm round

Mandy's shoulder. 'So far so good.'

She felt the tension ease. 'When will we know?'

'By the end of today, once he's started taking a bit of food and keeping it down, probably.'

She chewed her lip and frowned. 'Don't we know now? I mean, he's ever so much better already!'

Her dad led her to the window, opened the shutter and together they gazed out at the sea. 'I can't give you any guarantees, love.' He glanced at her. 'Want to come for a walk along the beach before anyone else is up?'

Mandy shook her head. 'I can't leave Kima by himself.'

'Hmm.' Mr Hope ran a hand through his tousled hair. 'A walk would do you good.'

'What if he wakes up and wonders where he is?'

They stood for a long time at the window, not knowing what to say. In one way, Mandy knew her dad was right. On the other hand, she would be worried every second she was away.

'I'll look after him for you if you like.'

There was another sleepy voice at the door. James stood there shyly. 'I'm awake anyway, so I might as well.'

'See, now you've got no excuse!' Adam Hope teased. 'James couldn't sleep either. Let's leave Kima in his capable hands, and I'll race you along the beach as far as the ruins. Get rid of these cobwebs!'

'OK, OK!' She put up her hands in surrender. 'I'll come. See you downstairs in two minutes!' She had to get changed first, and brush her hair.

'Three minutes?'

'OK, three. Thanks, James. We won't be long. I just have to show my dad I can beat him!'

'Cheek!' Adam Hope disappeared into his room.

'Back in half an hour!' Mandy promised. She was first into her clothes, first downstairs, waiting by the door when her dad reappeared in his shorts and trainers.

Their race soon turned into a jog, then slowed down to a walk along the smooth white sand. The palm trees cast long shadows to the water's edge as the sun rose above the mountain.

'Who won?' Mandy demanded, as she stopped to wait. She felt the warm salt breeze on her face, the fresh air deep in her lungs.

'You did; I admit it!' Her dad gasped. 'Of course, I had to let you win.'

'Huh!'

Mr Hope grinned sheepishly. 'Those were the days!' Then he yelled as he felt a wave lap around his trainers and splash his ankles. 'Serves me right, I suppose.'

Mandy ran to drag him clear of the next wave. Behind him, the early morning fishing *dhows* were setting off from the harbour, ploughing their way through a silver-pink sea.

'Is this where you found Kima?' he asked.

She turned inland. Without her even noticing it, they'd run as far as the ruins. Their deserted walls and crumbling domes made her shiver suddenly. She nodded, ready to turn back.

'No, wait a second. There's someone coming. Maybe we can ask what happened to the other monkeys.' Her dad took charge as he saw a silent group of men making their way on to the beach. They were about fifty metres off. 'They're heading for those boats. I expect they're going fishing.'

Mandy knew that these could be the very men who had chased the monkeys the day before. She hung back as her dad strode forward. What if it was the news she dreaded? 'Dead!' they would say, waving their arms as they had done yesterday. 'We killed the Poison Monkeys!'

She heard her father say '*Jambo!*' in his open, friendly way, saw the men stare back. 'Do you know about the monkeys who were here yesterday? Is there any news?'

The four men frowned. One obviously recognised Mandy. He said something under his breath to the man next to him. All were sullen and angry.

'Do you speak English?' Mr Hope faltered. He pointed to the outline of the ruins. '*Kima*? *Kima Punju*?'

He met a wall of silence.

Then one of the men said something in rapid Swahili. The words shot out as he turned on his heel and beckoned the others. They muttered, shook their heads, stared at Mandy.

'It's OK, we won't make any trouble,' Adam Hope explained.

'Save your breath, Dad.' Mandy tugged at him. All four of the men had turned their backs and were making their way to the water's edge, where their boats were moored. 'They probably think we're going to report them to the government for killing the monkeys!'

He sighed. 'Or maybe they didn't understand.'

'I wish.' She didn't think that was it. The men

were too suspicious and angry. 'Come on, Dad. Mum and James will be wondering where we've got to.'

There was no laughing and joking now, as they retraced their footsteps along the sand. In fact, they'd reached the small harbour before either said anything. 'We don't know for sure that the monkeys are dead . . .' Adam Hope began. 'So don't go jumping to any conclusions.'

'But what if they are, Dad?' Mandy narrowed her eyes and glanced back up the beach. 'If his parents are dead, when Kima gets better where will he go? What will he do?'

'I think you should come with us, Mandy.' James came out with it loud and clear. He sat inside the Land-rover, borrowed for a second day from the friend of the friend.

'Yes, go. I'm perfectly capable of looking after Kima, you know.' Adam Hope was back in cheerful mood, wearing the peak of his cap low over his forehead, peering down from the Nungwis' roof-top terrace.

Mandy stood in the street below. They'd arrived back at the house to find Kima nibbling at some fresh figs that Thomas had collected for him. 'Definitely on the mend,' her mum had reported. 'Thanks to your tender loving care, Mandy.'

'And James,' Mandy had insisted. They were in this together. She should have felt happy that Kima was over the worst. But no one could answer the important question; what would happen to the baby monkey now?

Doubt rooted her to the spot. 'I don't know,' she said now. 'I feel I ought to stop here.'

'What about the Black Plums?' James reminded her.

'You go with Mum and Thomas. Explain to Mr Pemba for me about what's happened here.'

'We'll be one helper short,' he insisted.

'Tell him I'm sorry.' She couldn't bring herself to leave Kima.

'There are lots of monkeys to move over the mountain and not many people to do it.' James could be stubborn too.

Emily Hope had checked the oil in the engine. Now she climbed into the driver's seat. She leaned out and looked up at Mandy. 'Are you sure?'

'Kima's fever might come back. I ought to be here.' At the moment he was sleeping again, but there was always the chance that he'd get sick again. On the other hand, she was letting the others down . . .

'What's wrong, don't you trust me?' her dad said with a wink.

'It's not that!' Mandy was confused.

'I know. It's a case of divided loyalties. You'll get a lot of that if you follow in the family footsteps and decide to be a vet when you grow up.'

She gave a loud sigh. It was worse when he was so nice and understanding. It made her blush. 'You think I ought to keep my promise, don't you?'

He leaned on the terrace wall and nodded. 'Leave me in charge here. I can have a quiet day all to myself, reading and snoozing and baby-sitting for little Kima.'

Another sigh, enormous this time. 'OK, you win.' She leaned over the balcony. 'Hey you lot, wait for me!'

Mandy ran for her stuff before she could change her mind. In two minutes she was scrambling into the Land-rover beside James, not looking back at the house as they set off down the dusty street.

'Oh, by the way, Mandy!' Adam Hope called from the roof-top. He was waving them off.

She leaned out of the window and squinted up at him.

'Don't go volunteering to help any more monkeys tomorrow, will you?'

'Why not?'

'It's a secret. Just keep tomorrow free, OK?' He grinned, then vanished from sight.

'What does he mean, "a secret"?' Mandy settled into her seat and asked her mum.

'I don't know. It's a mystery to me, too.' Emily Hope steered down the street. 'Now hang on tight. Mtondoo Mountain, here we come!'

'Uh-oh!' James listened to the cough and splutter of the engine. They hadn't been on the road five minutes and already the car was stuttering to a halt.

Thomas climbed down and lifted the bonnet. '*Hakuna matata*! No problem!' he assured them. 'In one minute we'll be on our way.'

'A loose wire?' Emily Hope suggested. She climbed out too.

They'd stopped by the row of fishermen's houses, Mandy realised. The shell of the big ruined house stood just across the road. 'This place gives me the shivers now,' she confessed to James. Even though the men were all probably out fishing, she wished the Land-rover had broken down in any place except this.

A car in the village was a rare sight, and it brought the children on to the road to stare. Women in bright orange, green and blue robes stood in the doorways of the tiny thatched houses. No one ran to greet them.

'See, they don't like us!' Mandy whispered. The usually welcoming islanders held back and gave them hostile looks.

'Can you see what's wrong?' Mrs Hope asked Thomas. 'Will you be able to fix it?'

He came and reached into the glove compartment for a roll of black tape. 'No problem!' he grinned.

'It's hot in here!' James hitched himself out of the back seat. 'Hey, Mandy, isn't that the same girl we saw yesterday?' He stood in the dust, watching a small figure in a pink dress walk towards them. 'Come and see!'

Reluctantly Mandy got out of the car. She recognised the faded pink, frilled dress, the tiny plaits in the girl's hair. 'I wonder what she wants!'

Everyone else in the village kept their distance, except the girl, who came shyly up to Mandy.

'*Jambo!*' Her voice wasn't above a whisper. She hung her head to one side and looked up out of the corner of her big brown eyes.

'*Jambo!*' Mandy managed to smile. The girl looked as if she'd been sent on an errand. 'My name's Mandy. What's yours?'

'Vastina.' There was no smile, only a worried glance over her shoulder at a woman who stood in one of the doorways. 'You have *dawa*? Medicine?' she whispered and held out her hand.

Mandy frowned. 'Medicine? What kind?'

'Aspirin. My mother needs aspirin for my sister. She's very sick.'

'In what way? How is she sick?' Mandy felt a knot tighten in her stomach.

'Here and here.' Vastina placed one hand on her stomach, one on her head. 'The monkeys came to the village. They have made my sister very sick.'

'That can't be true!' Mandy protested. 'That's only a story!'

James stepped forward. 'Can you show us?' he said slowly to the girl. He explained to Mandy: 'If your mum sees her, she might be able to work out what's wrong.'

It would mean visiting one of the houses.

Mandy glanced at the hostile women.

'My sister is very sick,' Vastina said again.

'OK!' Mandy agreed with James and went to explain to her mother. Soon all three of them left Thomas to work on the car and followed Vastina to her house, where the sick child was.

She lay on a plain wooden bed, on a bare mattress. Her little round face was drawn, there were streaks of tears on her cheeks. The mother showed them in, then stepped back out of the way.

Emily Hope nodded once and stepped forward. She felt the child's forehead and neck, lifted her wrist to take her pulse.

'Doctor?' Vastina asked Mandy, pointing to Mrs Hope.

'Not a people-doctor. She's an animal doctor. But don't worry, she'll soon find out what's wrong.'

Sure enough, her mother stood upright and came to explain to Vastina. 'Tell your mother that your sister has a fever. She must give her plenty of clean water to drink.' Emily Hope took a packet out of her top pocket. 'You must break one of these tablets into two and give her half now, and half in three hours' time. Do you understand?'

Slowly the girl nodded. She took the white tablet. 'Aspirin?'

'Yes.'

'What's wrong with her?' Mandy asked quietly as Vastina told her mother what they should do.

'She has flu.' Mrs Hope raised her eyebrows and sighed. 'She must have caught it from a tourist or visitor from another country. It's probably been developing with a sore throat and aches and pains for the last few days, but it's just today that she's got really sick.'

'She must have been the one who gave it to Kima, then!' James put two and two together. 'Kima must have come into contact with her before anyone realised she was sick. I bet she plays in the ruins most days, and that's where the monkeys came to eat the figs!'

'So it's not the other way round!' Mandy grew excited. 'The villagers think that the monkeys poisoned the girl. But really, she made Kima sick!' She was all for rushing up to Vastina to explain the truth.

But Emily Hope stopped her. 'Never mind now. That's not what's important. The main thing is that she gets better quickly. Let's hope the aspirin takes her temperature down and she soon gets over the fever. Maybe it's a twenty-four hour version and she'll soon be rid of it.'

Before Mandy could reply, Vastina came to show them out of the house. 'My mother says *Ahsante sana*. Thank you. She hopes this is strong *dawa* and that my sister will soon be well.'

'Tell her we hope so too,' Mrs Hope said gently. 'May we call and see her on our way back from Mtondoo Mountain later today? We can give you more *dawa* then, if you need it.'

Vastina spoke to her mother, who nodded. Then the girl showed them to the door. 'Monkeys very bad to make my baby sister sick,' she said sadly, glaring at the ruins.

Mandy turned. 'It wasn't the monkeys,' she began.

But Vastina's mother called her inside and she disappeared. There was nothing for it; they must go back to the Land-rover, between the rows of suspicious faces, who stared after them.

'Fixed!' Thomas said, slamming the bonnet as they arrived at the car. 'No more problems!'

They got in and were soon on their way.

If only everything were that simple! Mandy looked over her shoulder out of the back window. People gave monkeys the flu, and then turned round and blamed the monkeys. 'Life's not fair!' she sighed.

'What was that?' Emily Hope glanced in her overhead mirror at Mandy's strained expression. 'Never mind, we've got a busy day ahead. Let's just concentrate on that, shall we?'

Nine

They left the rickety car at Thomas's uncle's farm and got ready to set out on foot for the Relocation Centre.

His Aunt Manyara wished them luck. 'How many monkeys will you take over the mountain today?' she asked.

'Eight,' Thomas told her. 'All from one family. We had to stop on the way, so we're late. I hope Luke hasn't given up on us.'

Manyara stooped in the full blaze of the sun to pull up weeds from between the rows of maize. 'You're a good boy, Thomas. Luke Pemba sings your praises whenever I see him. He says he doesn't know what he'd do without you.'

Mandy was slinging her rucksack on to her shoulder, ready to follow James and her mum, but now she paused. 'You're not angry?' she asked.

'With Thomas?' Manyara stood up straight. She laughed at the idea.

'Yes. For saving the monkeys. I thought the farmers wanted them all dead.' This was a puzzle; Manyara was the first person besides Luke and Thomas who didn't seem to hate the monkeys.

Manyara shook her head. 'We don't like them, it's true. They steal our crops and make us poor. But they have a right to live.' She shrugged and bent down to her work.

'You really think so?' Mandy said eagerly. 'You're not just saying that?'

'Believe me, I'll be glad when they're gone over the mountain. But I don't believe the old witch doctor stories and I don't mean them any harm. It will be good to know that they're living happily in the east, and our crops will be safe too.' She pulled the weeds with her bare hands, bending from the waist.

'Do many people think like you?'

'Some, not all.' She glanced up at Mandy. 'You're the same as Thomas; you like the monkeys?'

'*Like* them? She *loves* them!' Thomas smiled broadly. 'But if we don't get a move on, Luke will think the leopard has got us!'

His aunt began to rake the loose weeds into a neat pile. 'Tell Jozani not to be late home for his supper,' Manyara said as they followed Mrs Hope and James up the forest track.

'Jozani?' Mandy asked. 'Won't he be at school?'

Thomas trotted along easily, into the shadows of the tall mahogany trees. 'This morning, yes. But this afternoon he'll come to the Relocation Centre to help.'

'He will?' Mandy's eyebrows shot up. 'Is he on our side too?'

'Don't be so surprised. We learn at school to take not so much notice of the old stories. They teach us new ways. And Jozani can make cages for the monkeys out of sticks and palm leaves. That's the old way.' Thomas laughed, his eyes twinkled. 'You'll see, we'll soon have the Black Plum monkeys over the mountain and safe in their new home!'

'How did he do that?' James stood back open-mouthed. Jozani had just shinned up the trunk of a tall coconut tree. He began to cut huge palm leaves and let them float to the ground, where Thomas collected them. 'Did you see him. He went up like a . . . a . . . !'

'Monkey?' Luke Pemba smiled. 'All the boys on the island learn to climb trees.'

'Not the girls?' Mandy asked.

'No.' He smiled again, this time at the strangeness of the question. 'We use the leaves for many things; to make roofs for our houses, to weave baskets to take the fruit to market. Today we need them to bind together the bars of the cages.'

He took a leaf from Thomas and showed them how to strip it and use the thin, spear-shaped fronds to tie stout sticks and make lengths of fencing. Then he took six of these, one to form each side of a box. 'We leave this side open on a hinge. This is the door,' he explained.

Mandy and James looked on as he worked, nicking the wood and cutting the palm fronds with his sharp knife. Meanwhile, Jozani came down the tree and began work on another cage with Thomas.

'We're not much help, are we?' Emily Hope apologised.

'Your time will come,' Luke promised. He

counted heads. 'There are six of us and eight monkeys. Can you carry a cage by yourself?' he asked Mandy.

Quickly she said yes, though when she glanced up at the mountain, she didn't feel so sure.

'Good.'

'But that's still not enough to do it all in one journey,' James said. 'We're two people short.'

'Not any more.' Mandy pointed through the trees. Up the hill came two more figures. 'Jambiani and Manyara have come to help!'

Jozani's mum and dad had finished their farmwork for the day. 'If we'd known you had so many helpers, we'd have stayed at home and taken a siesta.' Jambiani laughed at the busy scene. Five cages stood ready. James had gone to gather more sticks, while Thomas and Jozani worked on.

'No, no; the more the merrier.' Luke invited them to stay. He winked at Mandy. 'Luck is with us today; I feel it in my bones.'

'How will we catch the monkeys?' she wanted to know.

He answered her question with another question. 'What do they most love to eat?'

'Plums,' she said slowly. The monkeys'

favourite tree stood at the opposite edge of the clearing. She watched as Luke took one of the finished cages and took it across. 'Oh, I see. We put some fruit inside each cage and catch them one by one?'

He showed her how. 'Put the plums at the back of the cage. Leave the door wide open. "Come in, little monkey!" He spots the fruit with his greedy eyes. He's lazy. Why bother climbing the tree when a fine lunch lies ready and waiting on the ground? He creeps into the cage. Click! We rush to close the door. He can yell as much as he likes, we're not going to let him out again until we've taken him over the mountain to his nice new home!'

Mandy nodded, eager to begin. As Jambiani joined Thomas, Jozani and James at work on the final cages, she looked up at the trees, searching for signs of the Black Plum monkeys. She stared hard, but saw nothing, and today she didn't feel that she was watched by many pairs of hidden eyes. 'What if they've taken fright?' she asked her mum. 'Maybe they're too clever to fall into our trap.'

'Trust Luke.' Mrs Hope was calm as ever. 'He knows what he's doing.' She wandered over to the plum tree and chose some fruit. 'Help me pick the good ones to put inside the cages.'

So Mandy clambered up the tree and sat in a low fork, choosing the biggest plums. She handed them carefully to her mum. A flock of big, bright blue birds with a streak of orange on their breasts soared overhead.

'Maribu,' Luke told them. He'd come to announce that the cages were ready. 'We'll set them down around the edge of the clearing. Mandy, bring the plums and put them in the cages. Make sure that the doors are open, and hide the rest of the cage in the undergrowth. Good. Now the monkeys won't suspect a thing!'

Mandy was all fingers and thumbs as she pulled creepers over the cages to disguise them. She felt her heartbeat quicken. Everyone worked to set the traps, then followed Luke's orders to hide in the bushes. He made sure that they each knew which cage to look after.

'This is yours, James. As soon as a monkey creeps in here to snatch the fruit, you act. OK?'

James nodded. 'I shut the door and fasten it.' Taking a deep breath, he wriggled into the undergrowth behind the cage and vanished.

Then it was Mandy's turn. She was set to guard a cage underneath the plum tree, hiding behind a scented bush with bright orange flowers. Soon, everyone had taken their place and the clearing fell silent.

They waited. Insects hummed, birds sang. Mandy breathed in the sweet scent and watched a bee crawl into the trumpet-shaped blossom a few inches from her face. It was hot. Her face began to trickle with sweat.

Then there was a rustling noise in the bushes behind her. She stiffened, all her muscles taut and ready to spring. An animal pushed through the undergrowth, heading for the light.

Mandy prayed it was the first monkey, creeping forward to snatch plums from a hidden cage. It came close to where she crouched, then broke into the clearing. Warthog! She recognised the big head and broad snout, the bristly back and sticking-up tail as it stopped and sniffed.

She breathed out. The warthog rootled in the grass, her tusks digging into the soft earth. Then, when a procession of little warthogs followed, Mandy smiled. They were cute, mini versions of their mother, with the same funny, pointy tails. They reached the clearing in single file, then scattered. One turned and headed straight for the plums in Mandy's cage. What should she do? If the warthog took the bait, there would be nothing left for the monkeys.

But she needn't have worried. Just as the sneaky young warthog poked his snout into the cage, there was a loud screech. '*Kek-kek-kek*!' A monkey swung down from a tree and chattered an angry warning. *This is my patch*! *Leave my lunch alone*!

The warthog squealed in fright. He backed out of the cage and ran for his mother. Suddenly, the clearing was full of angry monkeys and the warthogs made themselves scarce. They bunched together behind the mother and high-tailed it out of the clearing.

Mandy grinned to herself at the sight of their rapidly disappearing backsides. *Now*! she thought. *Come on, little monkeys*! *Come and taste this luscious fruit*!

The plums lay black and juicy inside the cages. A bold young monkey crept up to one across the clearing from Mandy. Another, one of the nursing mothers, peeked into a second cage. They looked round warily. Who would be the first to try?

Then the old grandmother of the family came swinging lazily through the trees. She lowered herself to the ground and spied Mandy's fruit. She smacked her lips and poked

her face into the cage. Mandy was ready. She didn't move a muscle. She held her breath as the monkey leaned in.

The plums were just out of reach. The monkey crept forward and put her fingers around the biggest one. Mandy jumped out and slammed the cage door shut.

'*Yow-yow-yow*!' Grandma rattled the bars of her cage.

There was a chorus of cries and screams. At the same time as Mandy captured her monkey, Luke and Thomas had trapped theirs.

'Three down, five to go!' Luke promised, as the other monkeys fled from the clearing. 'We must be patient. Before long, their empty stomachs will bring the others back. Until then, we'll take these three to the Centre.' He was confident that soon they would have all eight monkeys safe inside the cages.

Luke was right. By two o'clock they were ready to set off on the hard trek up the mountain. Each of the eight cages contained a well-fed monkey, sulking quietly as it waited to see what would happen next.

Mandy watched Manyara lift a cage on to her head and hold it steady with one hand. 'Is that how we have to carry them?' she gasped. 'How does she make it balance?'

'Don't worry, we'll strap yours to your back,' Luke told her. 'It takes a lot of practice to do what Manyara is doing.' He chatted as he helped Mandy fix her cage to her back with rope. 'Not too heavy?'

'No, it's fine.'

The old female in the cage barked crossly as the cage rocked and swayed.

'Fine for you, not for her,' James grinned, waiting for his own cage to be tied to his back.

When they were all ready, they began the steady climb, out of the wooded slopes on to the bare mountain. Though it was hot, it wasn't steep and there was a track to one side of the summit. Mandy paused to let the others stream by and to watch the strange procession.

'OK?' Emily Hope asked as she passed.

She nodded. 'I was just wondering how Kima is.'

'Out of sight, but not out of mind, eh?'

'How could I forget about him?' Kima had been on Mandy's mind every minute since she'd left him that morning.

'He'll be OK,' her mum insisted. 'Your father will look after him.' She set off again up the hill. 'One thing at a time, Mandy. Let's just find a nice new home for this lot before we worry about Kima, shall we?'

Ten

'*Wah-wah!*' Cries of monkey joy echoed down the slopes to the water's edge. '*Ooo-ooo-ooo!*' Hungrily they scrambled into the fruit-laden trees.

'Happy now?' Mrs Hope asked Mandy.

She sighed. 'It's perfect!' The eastern shore of Kima Punju was unspoiled by roads. There were no houses, no farms, no tourists.

The group of rescuers rested in the shade of a giant baobab tree as the freed monkeys leaped and swung.

Mandy leaned her aching back against the tree-trunk. She gazed up into the dappled light, listening to a fresh sound. '*Kek-kek-kek!*'

'That's the Black Plums marking their territory,' Thomas told her. 'They're letting everyone know they've arrived.'

'Will they have to fight off other monkeys?' After all, they were the newcomers to the lush forest to the east of Mtondoo Mountain.

'No. There's plenty of food on this side of the island. What will happen is that the Black Plums will settle here, then they'll gang up with another troop, then another. Monkeys are friendly animals. They like to go around in big groups.'

'I suppose it's safer,' James said. He too looked tired. His fringe stuck to his forehead, his freckles had darkened in the sun. He stared down at the sparkling turquoise sea. 'Imagine swimming in that!' he sighed.

But Emily Hope roused them and pulled them to their feet. 'No time. We have to get back. I promised to call in at Vastina's house, remember.'

'And we have work to do at the farm,' Jambiani said.

Tired as she was, Mandy was glad not to stay too long. She took a last look at the Black Plum monkeys. There was one of the mothers with her baby, there was the old grandmother sitting blinking and yawning on a low branch. Out of sight, some young ones rustled excitedly through the leaves in their search for food. 'Goodbye,' Mandy whispered, then turned away.

'A good day's work,' Luke told her. He didn't seem the least bit tired, though Mandy's legs ached and her feet were sore. 'Now you can tell your friends in England how you helped to save the monkeys of Kima Punju!'

She plodded up the mountain beside him, head high in spite of her poor aching limbs. 'We can, can't we?' she said to James, a slow smile spreading across her face. 'We actually did help to save a species! When you think about it, that's fantastic!'

They said goodbye to Luke Pemba, who thanked them and shook them by the hand until they thought their arms would drop off. Then they walked with Jozani, Jambiani and Manyara to their farm. There was more handshaking. Mandy promised to write a letter from England. James gave Jozani his baseball cap. 'I've got another one,' he insisted. 'I don't need two.' Jozani's eyes lit up as he took the cap and put it on back-to-front.

'Come on, if we're quick we'll be home before

dark.' Emily Hope urged them into the Land-rover. It coughed and spluttered as she turned the key in the ignition. 'Provided this car gets us there!'

They laughed and waved, and were on their way, raising clouds of dust and rattling along. Mandy settled back for the hour-long journey to town.

By now all she could think of was Kima. Would he be completely better? Might he have missed her? When they had to stop to let two boys drive their herd of skinny goats across the road, she grew impatient. 'How long now?' she asked, half-hoping that her mum would forget her promise to call in on Vastina's family.

'Ten minutes until we get to the ruins.' Mrs Hope glanced at her watch. 'We'll stop off there for five minutes. That means we should be home by six o'clock.'

Mandy shuffled on the back seat and grimaced at James. When they drew to a halt by the fishermen's huts, in the shade of the ruined house, she decided to stay where she was.

'Aren't you coming, Mandy?' James had jumped out after Emily Hope.

'I'm tired,' she sighed. She saw Vastina come

out of the house to greet her mum and lead her inside.

'Come on, let's go and see!' James was puzzled. 'Why don't you want to?'

'Oh, OK.' Slowly she got out. Sitting in the car wouldn't get them home any sooner. And though she longed for news about Kima, she followed James to the hut.

' . . . Good, good,' Mrs Hope was saying. She'd tested the little girl's temperature and checked her throat. 'She's much better.'

The patient sat cross-legged on the bed, looking brighter than when they'd seen her that morning. Her mother sat next to her, holding her hand. Emily Hope spoke in English to Vastina. 'Tell your mother there's no need to worry. After a good night's sleep, your sister will be fine!'

Vastina translated and the mother nodded. '*Ahsante*,' she said to Mrs Hope. '*Ahsante sana*!' She kept her distance and didn't smile, but she was obviously grateful.

James nudged Mandy and took her to one side. 'When we get outside, I'm going to ask Vastina what happened to the monkeys,' he whispered. 'Maybe she'll tell us, even if the men won't.'

'No, don't!' Mandy panicked.

'Yes, it's better to find out for sure. Even if they're dead, we need to know!' he whispered furiously. 'If Kima's an orphan, we can go back to the Relocation Centre and ask Luke what we should do with him. Maybe there's an animal orphanage on the mainland. Kima might have to go there!'

'To a zoo?' Mandy snapped back. 'Oh, James, no!' It would be terrible to think of poor little Kima taken away from Kima Punju and stuck behind bars. She immediately pictured the worst.

'What else can we do?'

She closed her eyes and nodded. James was only being practical, after all. 'OK, let's ask!'

But waiting until Mrs Hope had finished giving advice was nerve-racking. Mandy watched her mum make a fuss of the little girl, taking her on her knee and smiling. The mother's face softened, but her eyes were still wary. At last, Emily Hope handed the child over and got up to go.

Soon they were outside again. Women stood in their doorways while the men gathered in a huddle by the water-tap. Everyone stared at the visitors.

'*You* ask!' Mandy whispered to James. She lost her nerve under the cold stares. She thought she recognised the boy from the day before; the one who must have run and told the men about the monkeys.

James did it quickly and simply. 'We want to know what happened to the monkeys in the ruined house,' he told Vastina. 'Can you tell us, please?'

'No.' The girl shook her head. She glanced over their shoulders at the boy standing amidst the group of men. 'I don't know.'

'But you were here!' Mandy stepped forward. 'You must have seen what happened.'

'No.' Vastina backed away.

'Are they dead?' James asked steadily. He made her look him in the eye.

'Yes,' she whispered. There was a long silence. 'Yes,' she said again, then stepped quickly inside.

Eleven

'Did you do as I said and leave tomorrow free for my secret treat?' Adam Hope asked. He sat on the roof terrace at Thomas's house with little Kima perched jauntily on his shoulder. The monkey's eyes were bright; he smacked his lips and plucked at Mr Hope's beard.

In spite of everything, Mandy couldn't help but smile. 'Why? What for?' She stretched out her arms to pick Kima up. 'What's this special secret?'

'Wait and see.' Adam Hope strolled away to talk to Mandy's mum, leaving the monkey with Mandy and James. 'And now that he's better, don't go spoiling that little chap with lots of treats. They're bad for him, remember!'

Mandy pursed her lips and tweeted at Kima. 'I wouldn't spoil you, would I?'

'Huh!' James was resting in a chair. He'd kicked off his trainers and lay back exhausted.

'Are you pleased to see me?' She ignored the snort and made pecking noises at Kima.

'He can't answer!' James snorted again, heaving himself up from the chair.

'I know that!' Mandy turned her back crossly. Then she sighed. As James shuffled barefoot across the terrace towards the stairs, she followed him. 'James, why are we arguing?'

He shrugged. 'I don't know. We've just had a fantastic day, and when we get back, we find that Kima's better. We should be really happy. But . . .'

'But?' Mandy handed the baby monkey to James for him to hold.

'I don't know. I guess we're just tired.'

'Yes, that must be it.' She gazed at the monkey sitting quietly in James's arms.

But each of them knew exactly what it was. It had nothing to do with being hungry or needing a shower. Nothing at all to do with being tired, and everything to do with Kima's future. They would have to face it sooner rather than later, Mandy knew.

That was the last thing her mum had said before she'd gone to take the Land-rover back to its proper owner: 'We'll have to decide what's best for Kima now that he's better. Let's talk about it at supper,' she'd told Adam Hope.

Mandy's dad had agreed. 'I've had a few ideas and made some phone calls,' he'd replied. Mandy had overheard through the open door of her room. 'I rang the animal orphanage in Nairobi. But you're right; let's talk about it properly when you get back!'

'Face the facts,' Emily Hope said kindly but firmly. 'Vastina told you that Kima's parents were killed. And now your father's found out that the animal orphanage in Nairobi would be willing to take him in. They could arrange for someone to come over on the ferry tomorrow morning and collect him from the harbour office.' She turned to Adam Hope. 'What time did they say?'

'Eight o'clock.' Mr Hope looked sad for Mandy and James. 'I know it's tough, but that's the way it is, I'm afraid.'

Mandy sat at the supper table, fighting back the tears. She'd already put Kima to bed in his box in her room.

'The orphanage isn't as bad as you might think,' her mum went on. 'From what we hear, it's more like a safari park than a zoo. The animals aren't locked up in cages. They have plenty of space to roam, and the visitors are kept well away. Kima will be kindly treated, I'm sure.'

'It's not the same as him staying here on Kima Punju though,' James said quietly.

'We're not saying it is,' Adam Hope admitted. 'But you have to accept that things don't always work out exactly the way you want them to.'

'Try and look on the bright side,' Mandy's mum suggested. 'Kima wouldn't be alive at all if it wasn't for you two.'

Mandy tried hard to follow their advice. She pretended to agree. 'We've done our best. There's nothing else we can do.' She admitted that it would seem better in the morning, that they all needed an early night. She went to bed as if she had accepted that Kima would have to go to the orphanage. But really her heart was breaking in two.

When she went to her room she could hardly bear to look at Kima, sleeping soundly in his box. He was so small and safe in there.

The muddle of feelings and thoughts crowded in. She just wanted to close her eyes. Would she sleep? Or would she lie awake all night thinking about Kima in the orphanage, lonely and lost? She crawled under the mosquito net into bed . . .

'Mandy!'

She woke to a knock at the door. Through the haze of the mosquito net she could see from the chinks in the wooden shutters that it was already light. 'James, is that you?'

'Yes. And Thomas. Come out here, quick!'

'What is it?' Hurriedly she flung on her T-shirt and shorts and rushed to the door. James and Thomas stood there fully dressed. Looking at her watch, she saw that it was seven o'clock. In exactly one hour they would have to take Kima down to the harbour to meet the man from the orphanage.

Thomas put a finger to his lips and beckoned her downstairs. 'Vastina's here!' he whispered when they reached the cool courtyard below.

'Vastina? What's she doing here?' Mandy followed the two boys to the big double doors, then slipped out after them into the street.

The girl from the fishing village stood waiting in a shop doorway. Mandy thought she looked scared. 'What's wrong?' Mandy asked, glancing up and down the street.

'Shh!' Thomas warned. 'She doesn't want anyone to know she's here!'

Vastina beckoned them away from the house. She cut down an alleyway towards the harbour and the beach beyond. 'Come with me. I want to show you something!'

They followed. 'Has this got anything to do with the monkeys?' Mandy asked, as soon as she could catch up. The girl had gone a back way round the harbour to avoid the boats.

Vastina nodded. 'I had to wait until the men in my village went off fishing.' Now she jumped down on to the beach and began to run along the sand.

'But you said the monkeys were dead!' Mandy stumbled and fell. She picked herself up and ran as fast as she could. James and Thomas kept pace as she quizzed Vastina.

'It was a lie.'

'What?' James cried in disbelief.

'I had to. The men hate the monkeys. They bring bad luck. How could I say they were still alive when they were listening? But I knew it was wrong. And your mother had helped my family. I wanted you to know the truth. So I came as soon as I could.'

Mandy felt her heart thud. Her mind was

reeling. 'It's OK, we understand! But you say the monkeys are alive? Where are they?'

'Here, in the old house.' Vastina stopped and pointed up the beach. 'They came back soon after the men had gone.'

'To wait for Kima!' Mandy gasped.

'It looks like it.' Thomas grabbed hold of Mandy before she could run up the beach into the ruins. 'Wait. We have to be quiet. We can't let the villagers see us!'

'But we haven't much time.' She tugged free. 'Show us where they are, Vastina!' She needed to see the monkeys with her own eyes.

The girl led them up the crumbling steps into the overgrown, derelict house. They peered up into the branches of the fig tree which grew up through the cracked floor. But Vastina shook her head and led them on, up an old staircase on to the first floor. They came out on to a flat part of the roof which was still mostly in one piece.

'Where are they?' Mandy whispered. She felt the breeze in her hair, blowing off the sea.

Vastina pointed across a wide crack in the roof. It was split in two by a jagged gap that was impossible for anyone except an agile animal to jump across. And there, safe in the far corner, sat the two monkeys. There were the same pale bellies and red backs. Their faces and hands were black. Their white ruffs of fur were ruffled by the breeze.

'It is! It's Kima's mum and dad!' Mandy cried. 'They've come back for their baby!'

Thomas stared at the monkeys, then laughed.

James turned to Thomas. 'What's funny?'

Thomas wrinkled his eyes, threw back his head and held his arms across his stomach. He laughed and laughed.

'Thomas!' Mandy was scared he would frighten the parents. 'What are you doing?'

The monkeys scuttled up and down the far edge of the roof. They chattered out loud.

'Mother and father?' Thomas cried. 'It can't be!'

'Why not?' Mandy looked again. It was hard to tell the monkeys apart; both had red backs and black stripes down the arms, they were roughly the same size.

'Where's the father? Show me!' Thomas chuckled.

She pointed to the one on the right.

'No. That's a female!'

'OK, then; that one!' She pointed to the one on the left.

'But this is a female too! They're both girls!'
He was enjoying the joke. 'One must be the
mother and one the aunt!'

'So? It's not that funny!' Mandy felt her face
go hot over her silly mistake. 'The mother and
the aunt; what's the difference?'

Thomas burst out laughing again, as James
dragged him back down the stairs. 'Plenty of
difference!' he gasped, catching his breath. 'Just
ask another monkey!'

They had thirty minutes to get back to Soud's
house to tell Mr and Mrs Hope the good news.

When Mandy reached the beach, she hugged

Vastina and thanked her. 'Look after the monkeys for a little while. We'll be back soon!'

'With the baby?' The girl's face was creased into a smile. Thomas's laughter was infectious.

'We hope!' James knew there was no time to lose. Already one or two women from the fishermen's huts had come out to hang newly washed clothes from the branches of trees. They glanced curiously at the excited children on the beach.

Suddenly, Thomas grew serious. 'I'll stay with Vastina,' he offered. 'You hurry back to my house.'

And they were off, running along the beach, hardly daring to think what might happen if Mr and Mrs Hope had already taken Kima down to the harbour. Mandy was afraid that the ferry carrying the man from the orphanage might arrive early. Then she and James would miss by a whisker the only chance to give Kima what he deserved: a life in the forest where he belonged.

'Which way now?' James gasped. They'd reached the harbour. And, yes; the big white ferry was already moored at the quayside. People came and went up and down the gangplank with baskets laden with fish and fruit. But there was no sign of a stranger in city clothes, no sign of Mr and Mrs Hope with Kima. 'Shall we try by the waterfront, or go the back way, down the alleys?'

'Let's split up.' Mandy made a quick decision. 'That way, one of us is bound to bump into them!' Her heart was in her mouth as James threaded his way through the crowd by the busy quay, and she set off down the narrow back street. 'We can't miss them!' she told herself. She searched to right and left, until she came to Soud's house.

Soud came hurrying into the courtyard when he heard her running steps.

'Have you seen my mum and dad?' She was so out of breath she could hardly speak.

He nodded. 'They went out.'

'Did they take Kima with them?'

'Yes. It was time to take him to the ferry.' He looked sorry, but could only shrug and look sad.

'Oh!' Mandy cried. She turned to run back towards the harbour. But she hadn't gone far before she bumped into James. 'Have you found them?'

'No. Haven't you?'

She gasped for breath, felt her ribs heave and her sides ache. 'We've missed them! Come on,

James, we've got to find them before it's too late!'

The crowd at the quayside still bustled to and fro as Mandy and James made their way to the ferry. Men loosened thick ropes and snaked them on to the deck, where sailors reached out and caught them.

'No, wait!' Mandy rushed on to the gangplank and ran on to the boat.

Men shouted in Swahili, caught hold of James and prevented him from following. She paused and glanced back.

'Mandy!' More voices shouted at her.

It was her mum and dad, pushing their way through the crowd on the quay, calling for her to come back. The ferry engine throbbed, the gangplank swayed beneath her feet. She kept her balance and went on until she reached the top.

'Please let me through!' Mandy came face to face with a stern-faced sailor. 'I have to find the man from the animal orphanage. He has a baby monkey with him!'

People craned over the side of the boat to see what was going on. They began to complain. The sailor folded his arms and frowned.

'*Kima! Kima Punju!*'

'Ah!' The man's eyebrows shot up. '*Kima Punju!*' He nodded and stepped aside, shouting orders to someone on the boat.

Mandy stumbled on board, not caring if they took away the gangplank or if the ferry set off with her. All she knew was she had to find Kima.

'Steady, steady, not so fast.' A man came forward through the crowd of jostling passengers. He was dressed in a pale suit with a white shirt and a green tie. 'My name is David Olduvi. I'm from Nairobi Animal Orphanage. What's this about the monkey?'

Mandy nearly cried for joy. 'Oh, have you got him? Don't take him away. There's no need. We've found his mother. Please don't take him to the orphanage!'

'Mandy won't rest until we take the three Fig Tree monkeys safely across the mountains.' Emily Hope stood outside Jambiani's farm explaining to Luke Pemba what had happened. 'She managed to get the young one off the boat just before it left for the mainland. David Olduvi was very co-operative, fortunately. As soon as he understood the new situation, he handed

Kima back. We took the youngster straight to the spot where his mother was waiting, there was a grand reunion, and now here we are!'

Mandy felt that she was floating on air. 'Pinch me, somebody!' she whispered. Three monkeys peered out of the back of the old, borrowed Land-rover; Kima, his mother and his 'aunt'.

'How did the villagers feel when they learned that the monkeys were still in the ruins?' Luke wanted to hear all about it.

'Not too bad,' Adam Hope said. 'As soon as they realised we were going to whisk them over here, they calmed down. Anyway, Emily is their heroine. She treated one of the children for flu, and now they think she can work miracles. They were quite happy for us to pack the monkeys off into the car.'

'Luckily they weren't angry with Vastina either.' Mandy's mother said it had all worked out well. 'We told them they should be proud of her. She's a clever girl.'

'And kind,' Mandy added.

'So now you're ready for another trek over the mountain?' Luke was all smiles as he went to find cages for the Fig Tree monkeys.

'I don't know about that!' Adam Hope looked

up the hill. 'Isn't that a bit too much like hard work?'

But Mandy and James pestered him until he agreed to come. The whole group set off, chatting and striding out in high spirits. By midday they'd reached the summit and looked down on the rich green eastern slopes. In another hour they'd settled on a group of fine-looking fig trees as their monkeys' new home.

'Open the cages!' Luke told Mandy and James.

Carefully they did as he said. First James opened the aunt's door. She peeked out and sniffed the air. '*Kek-kek-kek*!' She sprinted for cover up the nearest tree.

Then Mandy let Kima and his mother go free.

They came out cautiously; first the mother, then Kima.

'*Ooo-oo*!' The aunt called from her tree.

Kima looked up at Mandy while his mother went on ahead.

'Go on, off you go,' she whispered.

He seemed to understand, loping after the two grown-ups and swinging up into the tree. The last Mandy saw of him, he was sitting in a branch, his hands full of figs, munching happily.

'Ready?' Adam Hope asked.

Mandy nodded. 'Let's go.'

He put his arm round her shoulder and together they walked up the mountain. 'If we hurry home, we'll just have time for that secret treat.'

'We will?' She smiled at him. 'What is it?'

'Ah-ha!' He kept up the mystery all the way back to the car, and on the journey back to town.

'Aren't you ever going to tell us?' Mandy cried. He was the most irritating, infuriating dad in the world. She jumped out of the car as her mum parked it by the harbour, then headed for Soud's house.

'Get your swimming things!' he called after

her. 'And tell James and Thomas to bring theirs too!'

She turned, hands on hips. 'What for?'

There was a broad grin on his face. The joke was over, he confessed the truth. 'Oh, didn't I tell you? I borrowed Soud's *dhow* for the afternoon!'

'You did what?' Mandy's mouth fell open with a gasp.

'I borrowed a boat.'

'But you can't sail it! You don't know how!'

'Of course I do!' He shrugged. 'Oh well, if you don't want to come and swim with the dolphins, I suppose I could go by myself . . . !'

She gulped. He wasn't joking. 'Wait right there!' she shouted, while she ran for her things.

Dolphins, with their shiny backs and tiny eyes, their noses nudging through the clear water, clicking and creaking as they came . . . Her dad was the most wonderful dad in the world!

'James!' she cried. 'Thomas! We're going swimming. Come on, what are we waiting for? Let's go and say hello to our friends!'

Dear Reader

*I'm so pleased with the letters I have been receiving about **Animal Ark**. It seems there are lots of fans of the series, and I am very happy that so many people are enjoying the books.*

I especially enjoy reading your suggestions for new titles – so keep them coming!

Much Love,

Lucy Daniels

The Animal Ark Newsletter

Would you like to receive The Animal Ark Newsletter? It has lots of news about Lucy Daniels and the Animal Ark series, plus quizzes, puzzles and competitions. It is published three times a year and is free for children who live in the United Kingdom and Ireland.

If you would like to receive it for a year,
please write to:
The Animal Ark Newsletter,
c/o Hodder Children's Books,
338 Euston Road, London NW1 3BH,
sending your name and address
(UK and Ireland only).

All Hodder Children's books are available at your local bookshop or newsagent, or can be ordered direct from the publisher. Just tick the titles you want and fill in the form below. Prices and availability subject to change without notice.

Hodder Children's Books, Cash Sales Department, Bookpoint, 39 Milton Park, Abingdon, OXON, OX14 4TD, UK. If you have a credit card, our call centre team would be delighted to take your order by telephone. Our direct line is *01235 400414* (lines open 9.00 am – 6.00 pm Monday to Saturday, 24 hour message answering service). Alternatively you can send a fax on *01235 400454*.

Or please enclose a cheque or postal order made payable to Bookpoint Ltd to the value of the cover price and allow the following for postage and packing:
UK & BFPO – £1.00 for the first book, 50p for the second book, and 30p for each additional book ordered up to a maximum charge of £3.00.
OVERSEAS & EIRE – £2.00 for the first book, £1.00 for the second book, and 50p for each additional book.

Name ....

Address ....

....

....

If you would prefer to pay by credit card, please complete:
Please debit my Visa/Access/Diner's Card/American Express (delete as applicable) card no:

Signature ....

Expiry Date ....

ANIMAL ARK SERIES
LUCY DANIELS

1	KITTENS IN THE KITCHEN	£3.99	❏
2	PONY IN THE PORCH	£3.99	❏
3	PUPPIES IN THE PANTRY	£3.99	❏
4	GOAT IN THE GARDEN	£3.99	❏
5	HEDGEHOGS IN THE HALL	£3.99	❏
6	BADGER IN THE BASEMENT	£3.99	❏
7	CUB IN THE CUPBOARD	£3.99	❏
8	PIGLET IN A PLAYPEN	£3.99	❏
9	OWL IN THE OFFICE	£3.99	❏
10	LAMB IN THE LAUNDRY	£3.99	❏
11	BUNNIES IN THE BATHROOM	£3.99	❏
12	DONKEY ON THE DOORSTEP	£3.99	❏
13	HAMSTER IN A HAMPER	£3.99	❏
14	GOOSE ON THE LOOSE	£3.99	❏
15	CALF IN THE COTTAGE	£3.99	❏
16	KOALA IN A CRISIS	£3.99	❏
17	WOMBAT IN THE WILD	£3.99	❏
18	ROO ON THE ROCK	£3.99	❏
19	SQUIRRELS IN THE SCHOOL	£3.99	❏
20	GUINEA-PIG IN THE GARAGE	£3.99	❏
21	FAWN IN THE FOREST	£3.99	❏
22	SHETLAND IN THE SHED	£3.99	❏
23	SWAN IN THE SWIM	£3.99	❏
24	LION BY THE LAKE	£3.99	❏
25	ELEPHANT IN THE EAST	£3.99	❏
26	MONKEYS ON THE MOUNTAIN	£3.99	❏
	SHEEPDOG IN THE SNOW	£3.99	❏
	KITTEN IN THE COLD	£3.99	❏
	FOX IN THE FROST	£3.99	❏
	SEAL ON THE SHORE	£3.99	❏

ANIMAL ACTION

If you like *Animal Ark* then you'll love the RSPCA's Animal Action Club! Anyone aged 13 or under can become a member for just £5.50 a year. Join up and you can look forward to six issues of Animal Action magazine - each one is bursting with animal news, competitions, features, posters and celebrity interviews. Plus we'll send you a fantastic joining pack too!

To be really animal-friendly just complete the form – a photocopy is fine – and send it, with a cheque or postal order for £5.50  (made payable to the RSPCA), to Animal Action Club, RSPCA, Causeway, Horsham, West Sussex RH12 1HG. We'll then send you a joining pack and your first copy of *Animal Action*.

Registered charity no 219099

Don't delay, join today!

Name ....

Address ....

....

.... **Postcode** ....

Date of birth ....

Youth membership of the Royal Society for the Prevention of Cruelty to Animals

AACHOD2